"I didn't e Oliver," she protested

There seemed to be no way of convincing Neil of her innocence. "I don't even like being kissed," Petra added breathlessly, trembling with fear.

"No girl should make such silly statements, Petronella," Neil said mockingly. "What man could resist such a challenge?"

Perhaps because he moved so deliberately, Petra stood as if hypnotized, silently waiting. His hands slowly drew her close and he lowered his head. He took her lips slowly, lingeringly, with a punishing sweetness, as if savoring to the full all she had to offer.

Petra had been half a child until this moment, but now Neil had changed all that. It could only be a matter of time before her full awakening. Something smoldering in the back of Neil's eyes promised it....

OTHER
Harlequin Romances
by MARGARET PARGETER

Many of these titles are available at your local bookseller
or through the Harlequin Reader Service.

For a free catalogue listing all available Harlequin Romances,
send your name and address to:

HARLEQUIN READER SERVICE,
M.P.O. Box 707, Niagara Falls, N.Y. 14302
Canadian address: Stratford, Ontario, Canada N5A 6W2

or use coupon at back of book.

A Man Called Cameron

by

MARGARET PARGETER

Harlequin Books

TORONTO • LONDON • NEW YORK • AMSTERDAM
SYDNEY • HAMBURG • PARIS

Original hardcover edition published in 1978
by Mills & Boon Limited

ISBN 0-373-02241-7

Harlequin edition published March 1979

CHAPTER ONE

AFTERWARDS Petra realised if she hadn't been so busy lecturing David, her young brother, their mishap on the way to the Cameron ranch might never have happened. Fortunately she had slowed down considerably when the bullock hit them, otherwise the outcome might have been worse. David, at least, escaped unhurt, and Petra's own injuries, when she recovered enough to consider them, couldn't have been better calculated to help her through an extremely difficult situation had she planned it deliberately.

Nerves, she supposed, must have been partly responsible for the driving compulsion within her to brief David repeatedly since leaving the airport the day before. For an hour she had managed to control her uncharacteristic fussing, until they had left the highway. Having to travel miles over dirt roads had seemed to start her worrying all over again as, in places, the winding track had proved far from easy to negotiate. At one spot, where they had been obliged to ford an unbridged river, her panicky doubts had taken over once more and she had resumed her boring monologue of what David must not do or say.

David, usually the most patient of boys, had borne with her quietly for some time. Then, when his silence had driven her to ask sharply if he'd heard one word of what she'd been talking about, he had retaliated in his childishly precise tones, that had not yet been affected by their changed circumstances. 'You don't have to keep telling me to play dumb, Petra, although I simply couldn't remember even half of what you've told me, anyway!'

'Just so long as you don't forget we're merely touring Canada and have a great desire to spend a few days on a real ranch. And that we both would like to make the

5

acquaintance of our cousin. There might even be more than one of them!'

'And that we mustn't mention that we live in one basement room of a mouldy old tenement and that funny-looking men sometimes knock on the door so that next day we move on, if we can,' David mumbled stolidly.

'David!' Unhappily Petra hesitated. So he had noticed this, along with other things! He was almost twelve and she was reluctantly aware of his growing astuteness. He was conscious of that which she tried to keep from him, just as she had striven so desperately to protect him from the harsher realities of life since their father died. Since their world, as they had known it, had turned upside down.

It had only been a year ago, but seemed more like ten. A nightmare of a year it had been, a black period that had not necessarily finished despite the confident assurance of her planning. No, Petra pondered doubtfully, assurance was never the right word to describe the state of mind that lay behind her recent actions. Desperation might be much nearer the mark!

'I still can't see,' said David, when Petra did not continue, 'why, if we really are Neil Cameron's relations, we can't tell him everything right away.'

'No, darling!' Petra's clear voice rose, on what she hoped was a note of firmness. 'You see, we don't know— that is we can't be sure how he'll react.' She paused with a quick glance at David's puzzled face. 'I do intend explaining eventually, so don't worry, but even you must agree it could be better to get to know him first so we can choose the best way. He might be very easy to approach, but then again he might not. First impressions can be deceiving and it's not as if we have any real hold over him, you know. He might not be prepared to acknowledge a debt of honour. If confronted immediately with it he might conceivably show us the door!'

'What's to stop him doing that, even after a week?' David shrugged his thin shoulders without much apparent interest. 'Besides, Petra, I don't know that I really care. I'm not sure I'm going to like Canada. It's so big. I wish ...'

He trailed off, biting his lip, but not before another swift sideways glance from Petra caught the wistful look in his eyes. Sharply she bit back the emotional rejoinder that she, too, wished they still lived in a cosy English country house with most of what she supposed added up to the good things in life. Not that she could ever recall being personally too hooked on them, but until she had lost it all she hadn't realised how much she had taken for granted. There David and she had all the comfort and security anyone could ever have wished for, and, if it hadn't been absolutely necessary for herself, it had been for David who had never been very strong.

Her sigh frustrated, she looked at him again. Alone she might have made out, but it had proved too difficult with a young brother to look after. Nothing seemed to have gone right since that awful night of the fire, when their house had been burnt to the ground and, much worse than this, their father had died in the holocaust. Neither David or she had ever been able to guess how it had happened. Nor had anything ever been found to prove definitely it hadn't been an accident. It hadn't come out until afterwards that Charles Sinclair had been bankrupt, a man perhaps in a desperate frame of mind. Unbelievably it had taken the estate along with everything else he had possessed to pay his clamorous creditors. It was then, for the first time ever, that Petra had been thankful her mother had died when David was born. She had been eight when David had arrived and could still remember her beautiful, luxury-loving mother.

The time which had followed the fire and her father's bankruptcy Petra tried always to forget. The fire and its nightmarish aftermath, that had culminated in one horrible basement room—at least, after Redwell, that had seemed the only word to describe it! Then there had been a series of even more repulsive jobs because she had never trained for anything. Yet there had been nothing she might not have stuck if there hadn't been a man somewhere in each one of them, a man to whom a slender nineteen-year-

old girl's obvious virginity appeared to constitute an unspoken challenge.

If only she had been able to take a proper training, to
have been free to approach the right people, to have gone
through the normal channels. This way she wouldn't have
come to any harm, but for David's sake she had felt unable to approach anyone who might have helped her. A
weakly young boy, she was convinced, would have been
taken from her and perhaps fostered out. This, while probably admirable, was something neither David nor she
could bear to even think about. So, to date, she'd simply
run from all the bored, usually middle-aged men who
lasciviously chased her, always moving on, until the day
came when she realised she couldn't run much longer.
The supply of jobs was not inexhaustible and David began noticeably to suffer from the effects of too much
change and having to survive on often not even the barest
essentials. When his one pair of shoes wore down through
the soles she began to feel desperate. If they had any
friends she might have turned to them, but since the crash
none had wanted to know her and pride forbade her to
beg. If it hadn't been for the winning of a competition she
didn't know what she would have done. The money had
enabled them to make this journey to Canada, whereas
otherwise it would have remained only a dream. As
things stood everything could still come to nothing if
Neil Cameron wasn't the right kind of man.

Petra had known about Neil Cameron for some time
through her father's diaries which the family solicitor had
handed her after his death. They had been in her father's
London office, which explained why she had never seen
them before.

'Of no great value, in fact none at all, unfortunately, Miss
Sinclair,' Mr Brown of Brown, Holling and Spalding had
sighed regretfully, being fully conversant with her strait-
ened circumstances. Yet he had given her the name of the
well-known genealogist whom her father had engaged to
research his family tree and she had conceived the impression that Mr Brown wished to convey without the com-

mitment of actual words that this was something she could be advised to follow up.

Petra, to begin with, had been puzzled and not greatly interested. Enclosed with his diaries, which had been filled mostly with the dates of business appointments and meetings, had been a wealth of information about his ancestry. Why her father should have spent so much time and money on this she could not think, although to some, she realised, such a pursuit could prove absorbing. One thing had become clearly apparent—they had no remaining close relations, and his biggest expenditure had lain in the extensive investigation he had seemingly ordered into a branch of his family who had emigrated to Canada in the eighteenth century, 1799 to be exact, with the princely sum of five hundred pounds, lent by an elder brother of whom Charles Sinclair had been a direct descendant. There was no record of the debt ever being repaid. Indeed there was still reference to it in diaries which the genealogist had skilfully managed to procure and which he assured Petra were absolutely authentic.

'Impossible to prove,' Mr Brown had sighed when Petra had returned to him. 'Or perhaps I should say almost impossible to enforce, had your father such a thing in mind. I'll admit, my dear, from all the facts he so assiduously accumulated, that he must have had something, but I doubt if it was financial gain. Not for himself, at any rate. No such sum as this, even if proven, could have saved him.'

Again she had had the feeling that Mr Brown was trying silently to suggest something if nothing came to mind immediately. Perhaps it had been merely because she had no other means of filling the winter evenings that the diaries had continued to fascinate her. The Canadian branch of their family lived in Alberta where, according to present data, they owned a ranch which was run by one Neil Cameron. It had been interesting to note that their Canadian cousins must have descended from an unbroken male line while her father's had not. Occasionally she had toyed with the idea of writing to them, but whatever her interest she had had no fixed intention in her head to go any further. Not until she had won a few hundred pounds in the competition and David's immediate needs had become too apparent to be any longer ignored. As also did those of the man who worked beside her in the small factory where she had been fortunate enough to find a new job.

He had been watching her for days. Petra had been aware of it, although she had given him no encouragement, but it hadn't been until she had found him waiting for her after work that she had known real fear. He had grabbed hold of her in a horrid little alley, a short cut to where she usually caught her bus, and even now she could still feel his beer-laden breath on her face, his hands tearing at her clothing. How she had eventually escaped him she had never known, but she was agile in spite of her fragile appearance. Shaken, if otherwise unharmed, she had rushed home, vowing, as the thought wildly entered her head, that she would leave for Canada as soon as possible.

It had, of course, been a decision born of a rising hysteria, but even when she had calmed down and firmly taken hold of herself the idea had persisted. Would it be so very wicked to make one last attempt to secure a new life for David? She must manage somehow to get herself admitted to Neil Cameron's house. He was, as far as she could make out, a bachelor. More important, she had convinced herself, with the cold, unfeeling clarity she was reduced to, that he was a man with, no doubt, all a man's contemptible weaknesses. If the worst did happen she would sell the one commodity she had to sell dearly, rather than that part with it for nothing to one of the detestable rogues it seemed her everlasting misfortune to meet!

The money she had won had made an enormous difference even though Petra soon became aware that it wouldn't last forever. The change in David already after only two or three weeks of better food and heating was wonderful, but although she had been careful she seemed to have spent a great deal. Expenses had mounted so rapidly that there was now nothing left for their return tickets, should they need them, but this was something she intended keeping to herself for the time being.

As if on the same wavelength as herself, or possibly just glad she had stopped lecturing, David said more cheerfully, 'It's been good to have more to eat lately.'

'You've liked it?'

'Yes,' he hesitated, 'but only if we can really afford it. I wouldn't want you to get into any trouble. I don't really mind living in one room, you know.'

She forced a faint smile as she tried to speak brightly. 'But you remember how nice it was to live at Redwell? The house, your ponies, the fun you had.'

'I suppose so,' David's thin shoulders lifted resignedly. 'I try not to think about it.'

If, at the last moment, Petra had almost been tempted to turn back, the unconscious pathos in David's shrug strengthened her former resolutions. David had never been over-strong, and she should know, as hadn't she been with him ever since he had been born—or practically! Their father had even allowed her to go to a local school rather than a boarding one, so she could always be on hand to keep an eye on his motherless son. He had been away on business so much himself. The sudden transition from a country mansion with large grounds to a cold, sunless basement had nearly been too much for David. He had never got used to it. While Petra might have adapted and survived on her own, David's face, growing daily paler and thinner, had haunted her. For some weeks she had the frightening conviction that something awful would happen to him if she couldn't find a way out.

'Never mind,' she smiled swiftly, as David waited, 'you won't have to just dream of all the things you loved any longer. From now on ...'

Whatever her next words they were lost in David's excited cry, 'Petra—watch out!'

Too late she swerved to avoid a huge beast that appeared to charge straight from nowhere. With a wild, wholly terrifying bellow it plunged towards them. As, panic-stricken,

Petra wrenched the wheel around the animal lurched frantically across the nearside door, the impact stunning as the car took the deep incline on the right in what seemed to be a flying leap.

Petra had never been involved in a car accident before, nor had she ever driven a vehicle that hadn't belonged to either her or her father. She had had her own small sports model, in a beautiful shining silvery blue, for just over a year and this she had driven with care if, occasionally, too much speed. Since yesterday, in this hired car, she had been extra careful, but in spite of keeping to all the rules of the road this stupid thing had to happen! It was not her fault, but this was no comfort. It could mean—it must very definitely mean complications she could well do without.

Fearfully she raised her ringing head apprehensively from the steering wheel against which she had come to rest. She was conscious of some pain in her left wrist but, apart from this and feeling decidedly shaken, she seemed to be all right. Swiftly alarmed that she had not thought of David straight away, she swung around, opening her mouth to ask how he was, just as he did.

'We must look like a pair of goldfish, Petra,' he giggled suddenly, but she was aghast to notice that his face was white in spite of his humour, and that he was trembling. 'You have some blood on your face, Petra!' he whispered, his eyes widening.

So this was partly why he was so shocked? Nervously surprised, Petra belatedly switched off the still spluttering engine before raising exploratory fingers to her head. In the same instant she saw how the window above her door was shattered. It must have happened when the cow, or whatever it was, had crashed into them. They were probably fortunate it was no worse.

'Petra!' David's voice grew hoarse as she didn't answer, 'You're not going to die too, are you?'

Dazed, Petra looked at the blood on her fingers. 'Just a scratch, I think.' She tried to make light of it, to reassure him. 'It always seems worse than it actually is, darling. We could both have been really hurt. How do you feel?'

'Oh, fine!' David, now he knew she was none the worse, pulled a careless face. It was the kind of emotionless indifference Petra was coming to dread. 'My legs feel funny, but I expect yours do too.'

'Umm, you could say.' Petra had her handkerchief from her pocket and was trying to rub the trickle of blood from her brow. 'I think I'd better get out and take a look at the car. I don't suppose there's much wrong, but I can't see how we're to get it back on to the road, not up that bank, anyway!'

Awkwardly they both clambered out, Petra dismayed afresh to find her left wrist peculiarly useless and beginning quite definitely to ache. Together they stood back from the car, surveying the damage. They were at the bottom of a sandy incline, not a very steep one, and the soft bottom had probably cushioned their precipitous descent. It was quite obvious, though, that the car would have to be hauled out by a machine, that it would never make it by itself. It lay half on its side, like a small, drunken box, and of the beastly cow there was no sign.

'I'd like to tell the owner of that objectionable animal exactly what I think of him, but at least we can be thankful it's nowhere to be seen,' Petra muttered somewhat incoherently. 'Just what one gets, driving innocently along country roads minding one's own business. The horrible thing! I bet it's got an equally repulsive owner!'

She didn't really mean it as, instinctively, she knew to whom the cow must undoubtedly belong, but staring at their broken transport she knew she must either be belligerent or cry. The latter would never do! David, at all costs, must be protected from any possible worry, and he would worry if she were to break down and weep.

'Petra!' David's small, urgent hiss scarcely penetrated her consciousness, but his quick discreet nudge did.

Her eyes flew involuntarily to the road above them. Two men were there on horses looking down on them. How they had got there without her hearing, Petra couldn't guess. Maybe they had come up the incline on the other side and the sandy soil had deadened the sound of their horses' hooves. As she stared back at them her heart sank. They might have overheard what she had just said and would probably report it to their boss, who must be the man she was on her way to see. Not that she could make out if they were the sort to carry tales or not, as their faces were strangely spattered with mud, just as she vaguely recalled the bullock's had been. Having more time to study the men she could see that not only their faces but all their clothing seemed covered in the peculiar, glue-like substance.

After what seemed unconscionable seconds the two men dismounted, almost simultaneously, and slithered down the uneven bank to join them.

'You're having trouble?' The taller of the two spoke first, his voice a slow, deep drawl which Petra suspected hid some slight exasperation. Just as the lazy sound of him undoubtedly concealed much more formidable characteristics.

This last impression, fortunately, stayed just behind Petra's immediate consciousness, although she was aware of a faint apprehension. 'If you mean with the car then I'm sure you can see for yourself,' she rejoined coldly, her eyes searching in vain for some point of focus in his dirt-covered face. 'If your beastly cow hadn't pushed us off the road we'd have been all right.' She couldn't prevent herself from adding fiercely, 'Can't you control your animals better? You're probably paid more than enough!'

'I'm sorry, ma'am, or is it miss?' The man had his wide-brimmed Stetson pulled well down over his forehead, but Petra could have sworn a muscle at the side of his wide mouth twitched. 'The animal in question has just suffered the indignity of being dragged from a half dry waterhole. If it had been a lady it might have appreciated a mud bath, but this particular gentleman only appeared to be outraged.'

'You can say that again!' David piped up, grinning so cheerfully that Petra felt quite cross with him.

'This your brother, miss?' The tall stranger was evid-

ently weighing Petra up as his eyes lingered, as speculative
as hers had been, on her face.

'Yes,' she answered shortly.

'You've a nasty cut above your eye, miss,' he said next.

'I wondered when you'd get round to noticing!' The
shock she had sustained apparent in her slightly hysterical
exclamation.

'Oh, I noticed, right away, that both you and your—er—
car were in trouble.' His narrowed glance went slowly to
the pile of broken glass at her feet. 'But first I had to
establish how you came to be sitting at the bottom of this
ditch, miles from anywhere. Were you going any place
special?'

The bruise on Petra's wrist was really hurting now and
his questions didn't make her feel better. Biting her lip to
conceal a wince of pain, she said sharply, with a slight rude-
ness quite foreign to her nature, 'I don't have to explain
further, not to you, anyway.' Protectively she put a hand
on David's shoulder, drawing him nearer. 'If you would
kindly take us to your boss, who I presume is Mr Neil
Cameron, I'd be greatly obliged.'

From the shorter of the two men came a swift, if un-
identifiable exclamation which was swiftly stifled by a
quick glance from his companion. 'Jake, miss,' the tall one
drawled, 'is somewhat surprised, seeing how he doesn't
think the boss is expecting visitors. Not your sort, anyway.'

'No,' Petra's cloud-grey eyes widened, unwittingly apprehensive as she more humbly, this time, agreed, 'I'm afraid
that's true. We're his cousins from England, you see, and
only just decided to call. Not that,' she added haughtily
'I'm sure he'll be anything else but delighted to see us.'

There was a moment's sudden silence while the man, because his mouth tightened warily, obviously regretted
speaking so lightly to a prospective guest of his employers.
Even the shorter man seemed rendered curiously speechless as he did nothing but blink uncertainly. The taller of
the two was obviously the foreman, Petra decided, as he
did all the talking.

She must have been right as after staring her up and down, in a manner she let him see quite clearly she resented, he tilted back his head and rubbed one contemplative hand around his deeply cleft chin. His eyes were blue, she noticed, and the bits of hair she now managed to see were black. All of which pointed to a kind of positive personality. Yet, for all her rather vague summing up, she was scarcely prepared for the sudden decisiveness which seemed to bear out her swift impressions. 'As you're so sure Cameron will be delighted,' he said crisply, 'I'd better get you to the house right away, and get your car hauled out later. If you're staying there can't be any hurry, and the quicker you and your brother have attention the better, I'm thinking. Wouldn't you say so, Jake?'

Jake gazed at him blankly again for another second before mumbling obligingly, 'Oh, sure! Anything you say.'

'Fine, then,' the drawl was back. 'You take the boy and I'll manage Miss—What did you say your name was?'

'I didn't,' Petra said cautiously, not sure how far she could trust these mud-covered men. The line about not knowing her name! She'd heard it so often during this past year although, in this instance, maybe she was being ridiculous in objecting to it. This tall man, this drawling, taunting stranger could have no ulterior motives. He and his friend looked rough, however. It might be wiser to keep them in their place, if she did it nicely, and goodness knows among her father's so-called friends she'd seen enough of the art of patronising the lower classes to know exactly how it should be done. She raised her delicately rounded chin and looked down her slightly tip-tilted nose at him. 'I think I shall wait until I see your employer, my cousin,' she murmured, with a smoth confidence she was far from feeling.

'As you wish, ma'am,' he drawled back, too smoothly to be entirely to her liking as his hand went out and he turned her towards his horse.

She didn't care for the steely grip of his fingers on her elbow. 'Couldn't you send a vehicle back for us? I'm sure if you explained to Mr Cameron he would come for us himself.'

The man paused but briefly. 'It's all of four miles further on to my—to the homestead. I shouldn't care to leave you alone, entirely at the mercy perhaps of another rampaging steer.'

She blinked nervously. 'Was that what it was?'

'We thought it was just a crazy old cow,' David exclaimed, 'and Petra said ...'

'Petra?' the tall man cut in.

If she felt wary of being too friendly, David showed no such reluctance. He smiled and explained reasonably, 'Petra, short for Petronella.'

'That will be enough, darling,' Petra said quickly, too conscious that the man almost grinned, as if something afforded him some small satisfaction. Did David have to trot out her ridiculous name to all and sundry? 'I think it might be better,' she hastened, as if it had been David who had objected, 'if we did as this man suggests.' She stared at the horses doubtfully.

'I presume you've seen a horse before, if not a steer?' The tall man's mud-encased eyebrows lifted sarcastically.

'Once or twice,' she said loftily, now certain he was laughing at her. Her sore face and aching wrist allowed little humour and she refused to confess she had ridden almost before she could walk.

She had been right—he was amusing himself at her expense, possibly at the thought of her further discomfort. His smiled flashed very white against his mud-grey face. Why didn't he wipe it off? she wondered vaguely, thinking of the mud.

Currently absorbed with this, she missed seeing David taken up on the other man's horse until he rode past her. Then, so suddenly that a small gasp of surprise escaped her she found herself lifted and swung in front of the foreman. The smoothness and unexpectedness of the whole operation startled her, as did the tightness of the arm around her narrow rib-cage which caught her firmly back against the hardness of his broad chest while his other hand grasped the reins. Automatically her nerves tightened as every part of her cried out silently against the closeness of his hold, as the wild terror of men which had accumulated inside her rose to tangle incoherently in her throat. She was prepared to struggle, but was still trembling from the accident in the car and she realised, with some mortification, that without his arm around her she might easily fall off.

She shivered and tried to stop thinking of men generally, but didn't succeed until her injured wrist hit the saddle and she almost cried out. Stopping herself just in time, she held herself stiffly to prevent it occurring again and directed her thoughts towards the hired car. 'You haven't so much as locked it up!' she exclaimed. 'It doesn't belong to me, you know.'

'I guessed, Petronella,' he sounded more laconic than ever. 'Now who do you imagine is going to steal a crashed car in that condition, out here?'

'In what condition?' Finding herself cold with apprehension, she forgot to be indignant over his easy use of her nuisance of a name.

'Doors crumpled, wheels possibly twisted, windows shattered. I didn't look closely, but I should imagine repairs could cost a few dollars.'

Repairs! Petra's heart thudded with apprehension. Was it, was she insured against something which might be proved her own fault? 'If there's anything to pay then Mr Cameron must see to it,' she cried, fright making her reckless. 'After all, if he can't control his animals he must be prepared to account for the damage they do!'

Her voice spluttered off and she felt his long arm tighten, his fingers actually digging into the soft skin of her waist, yet his reply was not laced with any of the anger she felt in his hand. 'Steers and women, Petronella, are not easy to control at the best of times. Insurance companies usually take this into account.'

'Women?' she retorted. 'I wasn't talking about women!'

'No,' he agreed contrarily, 'neither was I. I was merely

pointing out that Mr Cameron might have more success in that direction. At least he doesn't have to chase them.'

'Oh ...!' Stunned into silence, Petra contemplated, the problem of the car momentarily removed from her mind. Wasn't it amazing what one discovered indirectly? Of course she might have guessed, seeing that she had known Neil Cameron was a middle-aged bachelor. As such, he wouldn't allow her to criticise the no doubt experienced methods he employed to enable him to enjoy to the full all the privileges for which other men were usually obliged to marry! However, if, as seemed apparent, this Cameron was susceptible to female charms, much as she shuddered against it, would it not make her own task that much easier? Exactly how, she declined to work out, telling herself evasively that this must naturally wait until she had actually met him.

There followed a twinge of disquiet, when, much as she disliked questioning this ranch-hand, she felt an urgent need to know more. 'You can't have many close neighbours here. Do you mean Mr Cameron keeps women at the ranch?'

The steely fingers dug cruelly deeper, forcing her spontaneous protest, 'You're hurting me!'

'Sorry, Petronella.'

Petra had a feeling he wasn't!

'I wouldn't want you to fall to the ground, Petronella,' he added glibly. 'That would hurt more.'

'I'm not likely to, am I?' she muttered angrily, 'seeing how you're holding me like a vice.'

He did relax fractionally and when he didn't say anything more she decided to let the matter drop. In fact she was glad to. It could be wiser not to pursue it. Now that her nervous excitement had subsided a little she felt a disturbing shiver of regret. It could have been better not to have passed several of the remarks she had already made. She could only think the shock of running off the road must have been responsible for such stupid indiscretion. Surely she hadn't come all this way to spoil everything at the last minute by not being prudent? She must learn in future to guard her tongue! This man on his splendid black stallion, with his somewhat comforting breadth of shoulder, didn't strike her as being the type to make trouble. Maybe she could appeal to him? It might work if she tried nicely.

In a small, husky voice she said, 'I don't want Mr Cameron to think I've been curious about his romantic diversions.' Her eyes fixed anxiously on David's small figure some way ahead. She must do better than that, for his sake. 'I'd be grateful, I'd even make it worth your while not to mention anything I've said.'

The horse reared sharply, surprising Petra. It appeared to be spirited, but absolutely under this man's iron control.

'You heard what I was saying?' she asked quickly when again he made no reply.

'No, miss,' he agreed eventually, his voice so expressionless that she had no clue as to what he really thought. 'Mr Cameron might be upset.'

'Does he get easily upset?' She forgot her resolutions of a moment ago not to ask any more questions. Well, she didn't exactly forget, but this last could be important.

'On occasion, Petronella, he can be quite terrifying when sufficiently provoked. But then if you're just passing through you are not likely to see it.'

'I see . . .' As Petra silently digested this the queasy feeling inside her grew, yet wasn't it better to know what she was up against? 'Thank you,' she breathed at last. 'And if he's sensitive about his affairs I'll certainly not allude to them. Poor man, I expect he's more to be pitied than teased. Being middle-aged and probably unable to find a wife could have twisted his character a little.'

'Ma'am!' The ache from the cut on Petra's brow was worsening, which might have accounted for the mildly explosive quality in that one bitten-off word. She was sure her waist would be black and blue from the increasing pressure of his hand, but instead of frightening this time it made her feel strangely safe. 'Don't you think,' he tacked on for full measure, 'you'd better shut up?'

Loyalty to the boss, Petra supposed, was an admirable thing. This man emanated it, with his respectful 'Mr Camerons'! It didn't please that he chose to call her mostly by her first name. Resentment smouldering, Petra quite forgot she had refused to give him her last one. 'Sorry,' she muttered, belatedly offering the apology for which he obviously waited. She would have needed to have been made of wood not to have felt the grimness moving within him.

He said nothing immediately, and, as she tried to shrug her stiff shoulders indifferently, she was again conscious of the hardness of his chest against which she rested. This, and the fragrant male scent of him which seemed compounded of leather and sweat. Wryly, not really aware of what she was doing, she turned her head sideways and wrinkled her small, proud nose.

He apparently interpreted her reaction to be one of distaste. 'You'll be telling me next I'm not as nice to be near as your boy-friends in England,' he jeered, pulling her, it seemed, deliberately closer.

'I don't suppose you can help it,' she mumbled, wanting to turn and glare at him sharply but unable to do so, clamped as she was to him with her head almost wedged beneath his jutting chin. 'You must work hard, but I expect you have bathing facilities,' she stammered, suddenly confused as she wondered desperately how such a crazy conversation could be taking place. This man seemed able to make her talk as she never remembered talking in her life. There was something about him, or something between them, she didn't know which. It was like a tangible cord against which they were both pulling. A mild hysteria seemed in danger of rising to Petra's throat again. Where were such stupid, naïve impressions coming from? What did she care if he never washed!

'We always have the creek,' he was informing her, almost as if he wished to unleash further indiscretions.

Fortunately she sensed this and bit back another too impulsive rejoiner. He could be simply passing a boring hour by baiting her. The countryside, what she could see of it through the gathering dusk, was wild, and they might still have some way to go. Curiously, for all he goaded her, she wasn't anxious that he would break his word and repeat anything to Neil Cameron. Instinctively she felt now she could trust him. The pain in her arm and head was beginning to pound and she still had Neil Cameron to face. First impressions—his of her—could possibly make or break the scheme she had in mind. She must conserve her strength, her wits, instead of wasting them on one of his cynical employees.

Cameron's foreman! Suddenly she was aware of his breath on her bare nape, of his hands moving slightly on her narrow waist, as if he would have liked to explore both above and below it. Her cheeks flamed and she went rigid again as her whole body responded in a wholly unfamiliar way, as if it actually enjoyed the sensations her resentful mind rejected. At once she told herself she was being stupid, that she was simply imagining things. This man didn't even like her, he had made this quite clear. Besides, didn't she intend selling herself dearly? Certainly not to any rough, mud-splattered cowboy, no matter how charming he turned out to be!

CHAPTER TWO

THE sun had long since disappeared behind the mountains by the time they reached the ranch. The ranch lay in the foothills of southern Alberta and Petra found herself continually struck by the magnificent beauty of the landscape when she had been expecting only rolling, treeless prairie. The warm, dry Chinook wind played on her expressive face as she gazed about her.

The actual house was something to surprise her again and caused her to draw a sharp breath. Set apart from the rest of the homestead, it was a long, two-storied dwelling with trees clustered behind it and wide lawns in front. These were fenced at regular intervals by white rails and posts, giving a neat, attractive impression. Even from outside the house spoke of comfort and a certain affluence, even if its rather formidable, sweeping lines hinted mysteriously at danger. Of this, along with the apprehensive fluttering of unsteady nerves, Petra forced herself to take no notice. Wasn't it sufficient to realise that her father must have been correct in believing Neil Cameron to be a man of means?

Beyond the house, as they approached, she caught a glimpse of other buildings, among which would be the bunkhouse and probably cabins for the married couples. From her vantage point, high up in the saddle, she could see people moving leisurely about, as if most of the day's work was over.

Then, as if hypnotised, her wandering eyes returned to Neil Cameron's house. 'It's—it's very impressive,' she exclaimed, with something like awe in her voice. The place attracted her in a way she had never expected to feel again, not after their lovely old manor at Redwell.

The man's voice behind her seemed like an unwelcome intrusion on her dreamy surveillance. 'You're impressed?'

'Oh, yes!' Her resentment quickly forgotten, there was no thought of deviation. Yet she was immediately embarrassed by her undeniably warm tones. 'I have—I mean I did live in a larger one, of course.'

'Sure,' he drawled maddeningly, 'I might almost have guessed. It's something you're quite used to.'

'No, I mean yes ...' she stuttered unhappily, wishing for about the hundredth time that she could stop letting this tall stranger confuse her to this extent. Thank goodness she wouldn't have to see more of him. Stirring uneasily, she tried to release herself from his arms as they swung around by the front door. David, she saw, was already standing on the ground waiting. Jake was back on his horse again and looking enquiringly towards them.

'You go ahead, Jake, I'll join you later,' Petra's escort gave the order, crisp and clear with authority.

Jake, after only a slight hesitation, obeyed, leaving Petra to exclaim hastily, 'There was no need for that! If you'd just let me down you can go with him.'

'Really, Petronella,' the man grinned dryly, 'you're in an awful hurry to be rid of me. Is it that you don't trust me?'

'Trust you?'

'Yes.' She could feel his mocking glance searing her averted face. 'You're afraid I'm about to repeat everything you've been talking about, should Cameron appear.'

'Of course I'm not. How ridiculous!' Intentionally she forced a disdainful note to her voice, although her heart beat fast with fright when she considered what he had said. If Neil Cameron did appear just what was she going to say? What would this man say? If only she could have had a short time to pull herself together. None of her carefully rehearsed speeches seemed feasible now, but she had nothing to put in their place.

'You could sound too adamant,' he drawled laconically, controlling the restive animal beneath them with a slight tightening of the reins. 'What is it you're after lady, I wonder?'

'All I want is to be put down!' Petra insisted, totally alarmed by something indefinable in his last dry observation. 'I'd like to get tidied up as soon as possible and my brother attended to.'

David, as she might have known, was giving her no immediate support. He was gazing around anxiously but obviously not in any hurry to do anything, or paying his sister any helpful attention.

'Your heart's beating like that of a captive bird,' the man mocked, 'I can feel it. I'm not sure you'll be able to stand on your feet.'

His fingers moved again, slightly upwards, and, panic-stricken, she moved restively. Whatever else this man lacked it wasn't nerve! David had turned towards them, waiting with the kind of adult patience that sat so oddly on his young shoulders and which Petra deplored. She found it rather frightening without quite knowing why. The man who held her followed her bewildered gaze and after a very few seconds slid thoughtfully off his horse before holding up his arms for Petra. The wince she gave as her left wrist caught his as she came down did not escape him, although the only outward indication he gave of being aware of it lay in the slight narrowing of his eyes.

From nowhere a young cowboy appeared and was ordered to take care of the horse. It occurred to Petra that this was why the man had taken so long to dismount. He intended coming into the house with them and he couldn't just turn the animal loose.

Taking no notice of her cold stare, he said mildly, 'I'd better come in with you. I can show you where to wait for Cameron. I'll see to it myself that he's with you very shortly. His old housekeeper is inclined to be deaf and might not hear you. Beside, she'll be cooking his dinner.'

'I see.' There seemed nothing to which she could reason-ably object and dejectedly she followed as he led the way through the wide door. David ambled after her, keeping close to her side.

The man strode across the wide hall as if he knew ex-actly where he was going. There was a thick carpet on the floor and the panelling on the walls had a lovely mellow sheen to it. A fireplace on a side wall was filled with huge logs, as if ready for winter, and a portrait of a man above it looked down on them as they passed. Petra glanced at that portrait in startled amazement. That, if nothing else, convinced her that she had arrived at her destination!

The man paused by an open doorway about halfway down the hall. 'If you wait here,' he said, 'you should be quite comfortable.'

'Thank you,' Petra whispered, wondering how he dared stride around them with mud positively dripping from his clothes. The poor housekeeper wouldn't thank him for it! Yet, despite this, she knew a moment of panic as he turned to go and had to bite her lip to stop herself from asking if she would see him again. 'Thank you,' she said again, her voice stronger, 'for what you've done for us.' She might have hoped for a glimmer of a smile, but not even a muscle moved on his mud-caked face.

Oh, well, Petra shrugged as she turned away herself, he might be right in thinking he had a grievance. She hadn't been particularly gracious and he must be the kind to hold a grudge. Much better to forget about him.

'Come on,' she cried immediately to David, as soon as he left, and the door closed behind him, 'I must see if I can't tidy you up. It really is important that we're accepted now. No car and obviously no kind of public transport! We must do our best to make a good impression, darling.'

Trying to sound happier than she felt, she was rewarded by David's tentative smile. Whatever happened she must manage an invitation from Cameron to stay, if only for one night. Suppose she had to go down on her hands and knees and promise anything? David, she could see, was putting on a brave face, but underneath he was as apprehensive as she.

'Didn't those men look peculiar covered with mud? I wonder what they are like underneath?' he pondered, his attention not wholly on what his sister was saying.

'Quite ordinary, really,' Petra returned vaguely as she searched swiftly through the pile of items in her bag for a comb, this seeming more important right now than David's idle queries. 'Not as ordinary, though, as we shall look if we don't get tidied up before Cameron arrives. Here,' she passed him the comb, 'you'd better use mine. Yours will still be in your luggage. I can wait.'

While she waited, in order to resist the temptation to tidy his hair herself, which she realised was bad for him, she concentrated on the room. It was of medium size and comfortable, as the man had said, with deep chairs and carpet and a fire flickering at one end. Against one of the walls was a mirror and she wandered over to take a look at herself. Rather startled by her own reflection, she stared into the shining glass. Her face was stark white, flecked with blood from her wound, and above it, looking entirely incongruous, there was still the large cotton square she had tied around her head. She had forgotten all about it, having put it on in the first place to protect herself from the dust and sun. Now she took it off, the pins she had secured it with being difficult to remove with one hand, but at last she succeeded, the release of the tight band worth the effort it had taken.

Next she dived into her bag again for a clean handkerchief, regretting the box of tissues she had left in the car. Silently, while David still tugged at his long-suffering hair, she scrubbed, attempting to remove some of the dried blood but not making much impression. If only she could have had a bowl of water! Eventually she gave up, deciding instead to concentrate on her hair. This she had plaited neatly that morning, binding it tightly, which could be contributing to the persistent ache in her head. With a sigh of relief she released it, and, as David gave her back her comb, she ran it through the honey coloured strands until they flowed in a heavy, burnished cascade over her shoulders.

She felt far from satisfied, but it would have to do. Her hair, if she kept her head bent slightly forward, would curve her cheek and neck, hiding the paleness of her face. Although the ache in her head had lessened fractionally the pain in her wrist would probably give her little respite before morning.

Again she tried to make light of it as she turned to

David, who, having obviously completed all he considered necessary, was watching her with what seemed to be becoming a habitually worried frown.' How do you feel now?' she asked quickly. Then, before he could reply, 'We are a pair of idiots, really. We arrive on Cameron's doorstep covered in bruises and blood. No wonder those two men looked at us the way they did!'

David's bottom lip wobbled supsiciously. 'I bet Mr Cameron won't be very happy to see us either!'

About to deny this lightly, Petra hesitated. David wasn't exactly a baby any longer, to be put off with a few inconsequential remarks. Protective she might still feel, but she must allow she could only deceive him so far. 'You're probably right.' Like his, her voice faltered miserably, and together, as if unable to find any more reassurance for each other, they wandered apprehensively to the wide window and lingered there, gazing out. This room appeared to be at the back of the house, facing the tall stand of timber she had noticed when they had arrived. From here, past the side of the trees, there were glimpses of the high Rockies, the giant crags and low foothills which sloped down to the plains. The awesome splendour of the mountain ranges seemed to be everywhere, inescapable, their blue cragginess broken on the higher pinnacles by white veins of snow, even at this time of year. Lower down the blueness of the rock was shadowed in places by the dark greenness of spruce forests and aspen groves. The tree line, Petra imagined it would be called, feeling a greater affinity for the mountains than for the vast, empty prairies below.

Yet while such a view might compensate for much, perhaps because of the continuing pain in her hand, other things obtruded. Thoughts of a hot bath and bed, in that order, took over almost completely. In a hotel she might have demanded them, but the most she could ask for here, immediately, would be for a quick wash of their hands and faces. Even before she met Neil Cameron the situation began suggesting things she hadn't thought of before.

Her brow creased as her good arm went, naturally caring, around David's shoulders, and so silently did they stand that when he did come Neil Cameron did not take them by surprise. They heard his footsteps approaching seconds before the door, on which their eyes were apprehensively fixed, opened and he walked in.

Petra stared at him as he carefully closed the door behind him before walking towards them. He was tall and big, she unconsciously registered that, but she was really only aware of fierce blue eyes under black brows, of a faint smile lurking at the side of his strong mouth. There was something frightening yet immediately familiar about him. He was like the portrait in the hall and the one she had herself. It was rather like watching an inanimate object coming to life, although she didn't think this man, with his decisively alert dark face, would welcome such a comparison. Undoubtedly he was Neil Cameron, an autocrat, she summed him up, to the tips of his long, steely fingers. She could take no comfort from the thought that he would be a man not easily fooled, especially when she must try to do so. His age? She suddenly realised someone, somewhere had been guilty of misjudgment. He would be in his thirties, maybe over rather than under thirty-five, but certainly far from middle-aged!

If she had been studying him rather closely he was doing the same to her. Black curved brows rose slightly above his cobalt-blue eyes as if he was no less surprised than herself. Forgetting to keep her gaze down as she had intended, Petra threw back her head to look at him, her throat, long and smooth, balancing her small head perfectly and throwing into relief her huge grey eyes and wide, soft mouth. Her brow above her haunting eyes was smooth and pale and her thick, lustrous hair tumbled heavily across her slender shoulders. Even in her crumpled, now dirty skirt, she gave, had she but known it, the impression of being supple and slim, her waist tiny, her legs long and delicately formed.

The silence lengthened as if Neil Cameron found the tableau they made, Petra and her young brother, interesting. 'I believe,' he spoke coolly at last, 'you wish to see me. Won't you sit down?'

Apprehensively Petra tried to smile, tearing her eyes from his smoothly expressionless face to grope rather blindly for the nearest chair. Her hand, which still gripped David's shoulder, pulled him along with her so that he remained by her side. If she had a peculiar feeling she had met Neil Cameron somewhere before it could only be because of the portrait. Or perhaps because his voice vaguely resembled that of the man who had rescued them? 'Thank you,' she murmured, aware of a flooding confusion as she scarcely seemed able to manage even that!

Cameron smiled again, enigmatically, as he waited until she straightened. 'My name, as you obviously know, is Cameron, Neil Cameron, but I'm afraid, so far as you're concerned, I feel completely in the dark. I've been told you claim to be my cousins.'

He did not offer to shake hands, which might have helped, but continued to survey them, almost as if they were a kind of curiosity he had never come across before. He studied them closely yet made no comment on the state of their clothing or the blood on Petra's face.

Strangely resentful, as she felt in need of the sympathy which was obviously not forthcoming, Petra forced herself to speak calmly. 'I'm sorry if I seem somewhat at a loss for words. No doubt your man would explain that we had a rather unfortunate accident which shattered us a little, mentally, at any rate. You really are our cousin, but I'm afraid I was led to believe you'd be older.'

'I see!' his exclamation was mild enough. 'Would it be pertinent to ask why you should be looking for me at all? It seems you have more knowledge of me than I have of you. In fact, I'll be completely frank and say I never knew you existed. I don't even know your name.'

Petra swallowed, finding his last remark incomprehensibly startling for some reason she couldn't make out. She was too busy regretting that she must be presenting the worst possible image! If only she'd had the opportunity to clean up properly. Other men had found her extremely attractive, and this without any effort on her part. Given the chance she might have made sure that Neil Cameron would have welcomed them in any capacity at all!

David, meanwhile, seemed to feel he must make up for his sister's ill manners. As he had done before, he said gravely, 'I'm David Sinclair, sir, and this is my sister Petronella.'

'How do you do,' Neil Cameron returned, with equal gravity. He shook David's hand but made no attempt to touch Petronella's.

Which seemed to proclaim louder than words that he doubted her story before it had even begun. Desperately, in a positive anguish of uncertainty and pain, Petra launched out rather wildly, 'You might not believe me, Mr Cameron—Neil, but we do happen to be your cousins and we decided to drop in on you.' The use of his name, like that, had taken more nerve than she had anticipated, and, from the way his eyes sharpened, it seemed he considered she possessed more than enough of it.

A light sarcasm crept into his well modulated voice. 'Maybe you'd be good enough to explain? I might add that I've never heard the name of Sinclair before, although I do know a bit of my family history.'

Petra stared at him, a peculiar feeling running right through her as her grey eyes met his, but she was too consumed with anxiety to take much notice. Her lips parted, words tumbling, eagerly breathless. 'I have a letter with me in which my solicitor confirms this relationship. He has all the facts. My father employed a quite famous genealogist whose findings coincided and added to those which my father had already gathered.'

'Really, Miss Sinclair,' his positive brows lifted again, 'you appear to have gone to considerable lengths! Why?'

Such hard abruptness did nothing to help Petra's hoarsely labouring breath. This man was altogether different from the one whom she had visualised. He was too ruthless—too young ..! Inadvertently she uttered the last two words aloud.

'Who is?' he caught her half despairing exclamation like a ball which he threw straight back.

'I'm sorry,' she stuttered, her grey eyes clouding, 'I

imagined, somehow, you'd be elderly and that it would be something of a kindness to visit you.'

'Really!' his brief ejaculation was slightly incredulous. 'I'm afraid you'll have to do better than that.'

'It was only an idea.' A sob thickened her throat, her distress something she tried to keep from him, in view of her future plans. 'My father, you see, went in for this kind of thing. It was a hobby. Otherwise we might never have known.'

'So,' Neil Cameron's sharp gaze went narrowly over the two of them, 'you were merely considering staying a night or two?'

'Yes,' she replied, too quickly, but not wishing to give David a chance to blacken his soul, 'something like that.'

'Something like that?'

'Oh, maybe a week!' Defensively Petra lowered her eyes, unable to sustain the impact of his any longer. Must he always pounce on the most vulnerable part of every sentence? He appeared to be considering this, as if he searched astutely for the more devious reason she sought to conceal. To have people staying, she realised, suddenly almost as shrewd as he, would not bother this man with his large residence overmuch, but to be deceived in any way would!

Fear, that he might be on the verge of discovering what she would rather he did not, made her rush on indiscreetly, 'You don't imagine I enjoy having almost to beg, do you? If it hadn't been for your stupid—er—steer it wouldn't have mattered so much, but seeing how it's almost wrecked our car I don't see how we can leave immediately. You must be about a day's drive from any other place!'

He nodded smoothly, his eyes on her finely flushed cheeks. Of a sudden, maybe too suddenly, he appeared to capitulate, as if her fiery indignation intrigued him in spite of himself. 'A town of any size,' he agreed, thoughtfully. 'It might not be convenient, but I do see your immediate problem and I suppose I could be held partly responsible. Not that I should worry too much about the car if I were you. Some of my men are already bringing it in, and I expect you're insured.'

Was this supposed to be consoling? It just happened to be one more thing she wasn't sure about. One more thing she had never anticipated. The car would have to be repaired. How was she to arrange it?

Neil Cameron went on, 'I suggest we leave any further discussion until David is in bed. At his age a lot of talk can be boring.'

So he was actually asking them to stay, or maybe he was merely permitting them to remain, which might not be the same thing! However, Petra thought, bitterly cynical, better one foot in the door than nothing at all. The eventual outcome could only be up to her. What had she to grumble at? She didn't realise that exhaustion was rapidly overtaking her, there was only a barely comprehensible feeling of being almost at the limits of her endurance. All the trauma of weeks of momentous decisions was catching up on her, their mishap with the car and the ensuing shock seeming to be bringing everything to a head. This, along with the additional discouragement of Neil Cameron not being as she had imagined him, turned all her prevailing nervousness into a fearsome terror which tied her stomach up in painful knots. Her face paled with the almost unbearable strain, her eyes widening, the pupils darkening before the cold-blooded appraisal of his. Helplessly she found herself agreeing that David was indeed tired and would probably be better in bed.

Neil Cameron rang a bell, which Petra presumed was to summon a maid or someone to see them upstairs. She hadn't given his staff a thought. He might not be suitably placed to have staying visitors. Before she could ask he stepped closer, his eyes keen again on her face.

'That cut above your eye, is it giving much trouble?'

'No.' This close the blue of his eyes was like a midnight sea and just as intimidating. 'It stings, but it's not actually painful.'

'I'll dress it for you when you come down for dinner,'

he said, as the door opened and an elderly woman entered.
He introduced her as his housekeeper. 'Mrs Allen will
show you to your rooms,' he assured Petra, as if it was far
from unusual for them to have unexpected guests. 'She'll
also bring you a tray of tea. I think this will be better than
a drink until later.'

Which made Petra feel rather ashamed at her niggling
resentment at not being offered anything so far. For herself,
perhaps, she wouldn't have minded, but David looked ready
to drop. She didn't drink much herself, she couldn't afford
to, but even when her father had been alive she had never
touched anything but a little light wine occasionally at
dinner. Still, wasn't it crazy—and extremely selfish—to
expect Neil Cameron to provide anything for free? There
was only a debt, which he might never acknowledge.

'I'll put your brother next door.' Mrs Allen stopped
outside a prettily appointed bedroom. 'There's a bathroom
a little further down the corridor.' She gave Petra another
quick glance and left.

No clues there as to whether she was liked or not. Petra,
looking after her for a second, shrugged, not having entirely lost everything she had been taught as a child—that
staff were to be considered but not taken too seriously. If
Mrs Allen seemed rather old and abrupt, there had been
someone very like her at Redwell. They were women who
had worked hard all their lives, who refused to be pen-
sioned off, and who usually ruled with a rod of iron. To
compensate for this their loyalty to the family was almost
always phenomenal. Was this the case here? Would she
have to be prepared to fight Mrs Allen as well as Neil
Cameron?

David's room was as nice as her own if a bit more Spar-
tan. 'It's a lot better than London,' he whispered.

'Yes, I told you it would be, didn't I?' Petra replied
quickly, almost as if she, too, feared walls could have ears.
'Look, darling,' she continued hurriedly, 'you'd better have
the bathroom first. There's probably more than one, but I
don't know where and I'd rather not ask. I'll wait and see
if our luggage arrives.'

David hesitated. 'Afterwards, Petra, do you think Mr Cameron would mind if I went straight to bed? I do feel tired.'

Petra glanced at him, frowning. His shoulders drooped and his face looked all angles. Anxiety sharpened within her, yet she managed to smile. 'Of course not. Maybe I can ask for something light to be sent up? I'm sure you'll be excused, at least this once.'

David was actually tucked up in bed when someone came with their cases, and when she returned from her bath she felt even more grateful to find the tea which Neil Cameron had promised. The latter she carried in to David along with the small bowl of fruit and plate of cookies which had been included on the tray. She was glad of these as she doubted he would still be awake before she could find something more substantial. For this one night this would be sufficient. It might be better for him to go straight to sleep. He was almost asleep when she left him, quietly closing the door.

Wistfully, as she stood regarding her small quantity of clothing, Petra wished she could have done the same thing, although the pain in her wrist was such that she guessed she would never have slept. She might have wept, but that was another thing! Resolutely she tried to pull herself together. To have got this far could be no small achievement, but it could, if she bungled things, amount to nothing. Having to change course in mid-stream was in itself no easy matter. She had come all set to charm a fatherly figure, or at least someone older, perhaps malleable and lonely. While Neil Cameron might be in his thirties this was far from being elderly, and if he did live by himself he would never, she was convinced, be lonely! Not for feminine company, anyway. Tall and broad-shouldered with a lean, hard body, he was certainly attractive. While she wasn't sure she liked such blatant masculinity, Petra realised most women would find him exciting, and he looked as if he found them easy game. His mouth was sensuous and she had the distinct impression he did more than speak with it!

A quiver of feeling, like a crackling vibration, hit Petra

sharply, moving right through her, a pain to accentuate
the already throbbing one in her wrist. Now she realised
why she couldn't think of him as a stranger. He was the
image of that earlier Cameron whose cleverly painted likeness had hung in her father's study for so long. Charles
Sinclair had never had any clear idea where it had come
from other than that it had been stacked away with a lot
of old junk which had been cleared from his grandfather's
attics when he'd died. He had known only that it was one of
his Scottish ancestors. Petra remembered how, years ago,
her mother had banished it to her father's study, declaring
laughingly but with determination that it was too strong
a face for daily perusal, and as no one was at all conversant
with the man's history it surely couldn't matter where he
hung.

But it had mattered, in some strange indefinable way, to
the young Petronella. Even then she had found that face,
which gazed so proudly beyond her head with such dark
blue eyes, oddly fascinating. In later years she had been
much given to a more furtive contemplation of it, spending time in the study while no one was there staring at it
earnestly. Over the years she had become quite fascinated
by the strength of those hard-hewed features, the arrogant
set of his head. She had began to weave dreams around
him even while she had tried to keep a sense of proportion,
aware that it could only be foolish to become so fascinated
by someone no longer alive. It might make people laugh at
her, if nothing else.

Yet when her father had parcelled it up and taken it to
London she had been desolate. It had happened about a
year before he died. He had said it was to have it cleaned
and valued and given all sorts of excuses for not bringing
it back. Petra had asked so often, but like a young girl in
the throes of her first love affair, she had selfconsciously
not dared to insist. After the fire, when it had been returned by the genealogist, she had realised that if it hadn't
been there she would have lost it for ever.

It had been the one thing from the wreck of her father's
business she had had no scruples about taking. Whether it

was worth five pounds or five thousand—which she doubted—she had no intention of handing it over. Deliberately she had told no one about it, keeping it for herself. It had been something of a shock to find its replica in the hall of a ranch-house, but not so devastating as the one she had received on meeting Neil Cameron in person.

Meeting him had been like seeing someone, quite literally, step down from a wall, out of a painting. A painting she had grown perhaps unreasonably attached to. Somehow, in her mind, she must separate the living Cameron from the one of her dreams, yet how was she to do so when he seemed only a harder, more ruthless version of the one in the portrait?

How Petra wished at that moment for someone she could have confided in. Even the man on whose horse she had arrived seemed oddly comforting compared with Neil Cameron. She must make enquiries about that man, his foreman. In spite of his coolness and mockery his arms had been strongly protective, and she might need a friend here.

Swiftly, while her mind considered and struggled with her increasing problems, she drew from her case a long skirt and the silky top that went with it. As they had travelled by air she intended making this an excuse to justify the smallness of her wardrobe. She hoped no one would notice the cheapness of it. There was only a pair of jeans and a skirt, apart from this skirt and another dress for evening wear, and she might not have had these if she hadn't managed to purchase them for next to nothing in an early summer sale. As she slipped the blue blouse over her head and belted the badly cut black skirt to her narrow waist, she thought ruefully of the beautiful clothes she had once owned, which had all been destroyed in the fire. Those days, however, were gone for ever and no amount of longing would bring them back. She could only pray that Neil Cameron was no authority on women's clothes, so he wouldn't notice if she wore the same thing night after night. Always assuming she could make sure there was to be a continuation of nights!

The frightening suspicion that she could be on her way tomorrow strengthened her apprehensive conviction that she must do everything she could to charm Neil Cameron. Her face, even without make-up, was nothing to be ashamed of, but she had been taught how to make the most of it in the expensive school she had attended. A little extra allure now might not come amiss, but it was difficult to manage satisfactorily with only one good hand. Her left she still couldn't move without considerable pain and while, with her other one, she could brush her long hair she was unable to tie it back. Attempting to obtain a small dab of foundation, she managed to spill half of it and could have wept to see the precious fluid spread over the dressing table instead of her skin. With a tissue she hastily mopped it up, having an inbred respect for beautiful things, and the wood of this bedroom suite was indeed lovely. Eventually she succeeded in getting a little of everything on to her face, then, tidying all her paraphernalia carefully away, she stole downstairs after looking in again on a still sleeping David.

Neil Cameron was standing in the hall as she came down and she was surprised to find him there. He might be polite to unexpected guests, even those who claimed to be cousins, but she had not thought he would put himself out. As his eyes followed her progress closely she almost stumbled on the last tread. Grasping the open rail unwittingly with her injured arm, she could scarcely stop herself from crying out. Her teeth sank into her bottom lip and her cheeks whitened beneath his sharpening regard.

'I merely waited to show you into the lounge while Mrs Allen puts the finishing touches to our dinner. I'm not so terrifying, surely, that you should go pale at the sight of me, Miss Sinclair?'

Dismay fluttered Petra's long lashes uncertainly. If he was convinced he really was her cousin would he have called her that? 'I wasn't aware I had gone pale, Neil.' Ignoring an unbearable impulse to nurse her sore hand, she deliberately chose to address him thus, hoping it would give the impression that the doubt was all on his side.

His smile glinted as he walked towards her without once removing the lancing penetration of his eyes. 'Whatever your—er—accomplishments, you don't lie easily, my dear. Let me see your hand. When you clutched the rail you positively winced. You could have hurt yourself more than you realised when your car ran off the track.'

'No.'

'Isn't it childish to put your hand behind your back?'

It might be, but she wouldn't admit it. In spite of his more favourable expression she didn't like his tones. Momentarily she forgot she must do her best to impress him. 'I've told you, I'm all right!'

'Let me be the judge of that.'

Rather desperately her eyes darted sideways. 'You've a very nice house.'

'Petronella!'

'As you wish,' she capitulated dully. Yet, perversely, it wasn't her hand she stared at as she drew it out reluctantly; her violet-shadowed gaze was riveted on his threatening face. There it was again, the strange feeling of familiarity, as if she had known this man a long, long time and long ago. Drat that portrait, inwardly she panicked, the small tremor going through her betrayed by her sharply drawn breath. This Cameron was living and breathing flesh, so much more than a mere painting on a wall!

His eyes glittered as he took hold of her hand and this time there was no mistaking her small whimper of pain. 'I thought as much!' His exclamation was uttered over a swift examination of her wrist, as he experimentally but very gently flexed her long, fragile fingers. 'Why didn't you mention this?'

She said a little distractedly, oddly affected by the touch of him, more than by the pain in her hand, 'I didn't think —I still don't think it's anything to make a fuss over. I've probably wrenched it. I should imagine it will be completely recovered by morning.'

His eyes once more raked her gently perspiring face, and he seemed quite unimpressed by any show of bravery. 'I'd better put a bandage on this before you pass out on me. In the morning I shall take you to see a doctor, if I deem it necessary.'

'Oh, no!' Swiftly, a panicky pulse beating hard against the softness of her throat, she tried to pull away. A doctor here would cost the earth and she didn't have that kind of money. Scarcely any money at all—if she had to think about it!

'Why not?' His eyes still clamped coolly on her. 'It won't be a big thing, if it's money you're worrying about. In any case, you must be insured against such mishaps.'

'The car, you mean?'

'No, medically.'

'I ...' Her eyes huge in her shaken white face, Petra hesitated. Why confess when she might easily recover without out professional treatment? Neil Cameron, she suspected, would be something of an expert with a medical kit, living in such isolation out here. 'If you could put a small bandage around it, I'm sure I'll recover,' she said.

His white teeth snapped together, as if in exasperation, but he didn't press the issue. He merely took her other arm and led her down the hallway. 'It won't take a minute,' he assured her smoothly. 'I'd better tell Mrs Allen to see to your young brother when he comes down or he'll wonder where we've got to.'

'I'm afraid,' Petra confessed, 'he's gone to sleep. He was tired. You see he is not very strong.'

'Or you probably pamper him too much,' came the noticeably unsympathetic reply. 'Sisters and mothers are always doing it.'

Petra was thinking how to point out politely that he must have had at least a mother himself, when he added curtly, 'It's perhaps as well David has gone early to bed because, as I suggested before, you and I have quite a lot to talk about.'

CHAPTER THREE

'How old is your brother, Petronella?' Neil Cameron enquired before they had taken many more steps. The clasp of his fingers under her arm hardened a little, as if he was finding the situation called for more patience than he was willing to expend.

'He's almost twelve, I'm twenty,' Petra obliged quickly, wishing him in a more amiable mood and feeling the only way to achieve this was to humour him. It must be a favourable sign that he had called her Petronella for the second time.

'Most people call me Petra,' she told him, with a dazzling smile. 'It's quicker.'

'I'm in no hurry where you're concerned,' he drawled, his eyes sardonically on her face which her smile transformed into something memorable. 'It appears I have two uninvited guests, one still in and the other barely out of the schoolroom. Can you wonder if I've decided to take my time?'

Two guests! So he wasn't yet ready to concede any relationship? Silently she accompanied him into a small, clinically spotless room which contained, along with other things, what seemed to be a large medicine cupboard.

'Sit down at the table while I find a suitable bandage,' he ordered.

Firmly he examined her wrist again before applying it. 'I could guess you've wrenched it rather badly, but this should give you some relief. If nothing else it will relieve the pain.' In spite of his astringent tones his hands were infinitely gentle as he wound the soft crêpe firmly and, as he had assured her, she immediately felt better. 'Move it as little as possible for a day or two,' he advised. 'It could mean you'll have to postpone moving on, but a couple of days won't hurt me.'

'Thank you,' she breathed, a current of resentment bringing faint colour to her pale cheeks as she tried to ignore
his derisive last word. He didn't believe in pulling his
punches! He was a man who had no hesitation when it
came to speaking his mind, no compunction about sparing
a girl's feelings!

He didn't talk much during dinner, and Petra, once the
ache in her wrist and temper subsided, found herself almost
unashamedly revelling in the nearly forgotten pleasures of
gleaming silver and crystal. The table was long, with oval
ends, giving the impression that Neil Cameron might use
it often for entertaining. Everything was exactly as it
should be, she couldn't fault any of it. The porcelain was
of the best quality, the dining-room beautifully appointed,
even the wine was at the correct temperature, clear and
sparkling. It all reminded her too poignantly of Redwell
before the crash, but her experience there enabled her to
conduct herself unselfconsciously tonight, very much like
the chatelaine of a large house, a role she had often taken,
at her father's request, in place of her mother. Petra had
expected to eat well. According to the information she had
Neil Cameron was not a poor man, but she hadn't visualised anything like this! A scrubbed kitchen table, perhaps,
or a comfortable, shabby front parlour, like something out
of an old-fashioned Western film, but nothing like the
degree of luxury she found here. She lapped it up greedily,
her enjoyment of it, for all her cool little front, so pathetic-
ally obvious that the eyes of the man sitting opposite narrowed increasingly.

Unaware that she aroused some suspicion, Petra carried
on dreamily. The bandage and tablets Neil Cameron had
given her had taken almost all the pain from her injured
wrist and she managed her meal wonderfully well with one
hand. Softly, as her immediate worries retreated slightly
beneath so much affluence, she smiled at him. After all, he
was only a man, and she had learnt, if painfully, during
the last year that men were strangely susceptible to her
smiles.

He poured her more wine, marvellously accurate, seeing

how he scarcely took his eyes from her face. 'You feel better now?'

If she had been lost in an impracticably rosy glow, his dry query cruelly dispelled it. Her eyes fastened on his as she flushed guiltily, but she could read nothing in the studied blank depth she encountered. 'Yes, thank you,' she murmured, as if she suddenly found the sight of him in his casual but well-cut clothes rather overwhelming. She opened her mouth to attempt something more original, but he forestalled her.

'Finish your wine, Petronella,' he said relentlessly, his hard voice gently mocking. 'We'll have coffee in the lounge. You've had a long day and may have to face an even longer few minutes. It all depends what you have on your mind.'

What was on his, more likely! Defensively Petra lowered her too expressive eyes as she controlled, with difficulty, a sharp retort. How humiliating it was to remember she wasn't really in a position to do anything else but crawl! One wrong word on her part and all her plans could come to nought. Not for her the wonderful release of being able to speak her mind. Convincing Neil Cameron of her exact identity might be comparatively easy, it was the next step which would take every scrap of her ingenuity. By that time she must have him almost begging her to stay. And because she had, as yet, no positive idea as to how she would go about it she decided she would concentrate, this evening, on the first stage of his submission.

The lounge, to her delight, was even nicer than the dining-room. It was a large room, closely fitted with deep carpeting and there were low, comfortable chairs. A light breeze, still warm, slid in through the open windows, bringing with it a faint aroma of something she could put no name to. Whatever it was, it was sweet and had an odd effect on the senses, but then she had always been susceptible to sensuous scents, borne on the wind.

Quickly she turned away from the enticing windows and sat down, unknowingly bracing her slender shoulders as if preparing to face an inquisition. Mrs Allen brought in their coffee, but Neil Cameron asked Petra to pour it, neatly, she realised, seconds later, giving himself the initiative.

'You say you have proof you're my cousin? I find this intriguing, if hard to believe.'

His deep voice, so suddenly sharpening, induced fright. The coffee pot wobbled as she almost spilt the hot liquid over her hand.

'Careful!' his cool warning stung. 'One might almost imagine you're in no way convinced yourself?'

'Oh, but I am!' Hastily she checked, for fear she sounded too eager. 'I told you before I have all the proof anyone could ask for. I also have a portrait.'

'Portrait?' Carefully controlled interest was allowed to enter his dark eyes, as they surveyed her glowing cheeks.

'An exact replica of the one that hangs in your hall!'

He paused a brief second, letting her enjoy a momentary triumph. 'Where do you have yours? I presume you conveniently forgot to bring it along with you. You left it at home?'

This time colour really flooded her face. That last sentence seemed to betray that he thought her a scheming hussy. 'You're——' Dismayed, Petra paused. She'd been about to say, despicable!

'Why don't you—say it?' he taunted softly, the degree of intimacy something she found difficult to adjust to. 'It really gets me, Petronella, the way you continually hold back. I wouldn't be half as suspicious if you really let go.'

How could she? How she wished she dared, but she could not! Because wasn't she just as contriving as he thought? 'I do have a portrait,' she cried, jumping to her feet, ignoring her conscience. 'It's upstairs, I'll go and get it if you'll wait!'

'Oh, I'll do that,' he drawled, lowering his tall, lithe body down into a chair where he stretched pantherishly. 'This gets more engrossing by the minute. Maybe my jaded senses are in need of such stimulation.'

Whatever he meant by this, Petra didn't stop to ask. Swiftly she left him, her feet barely touching the carpet as

she ran upstairs, returning breathlessly with what she considered to be the indisputable proof of her own identity.
The painting she clasped to her breast, almost as if afraid
he was about to snatch it from her.

'Let me have it.' Now his drawl was quite pleasant as he
came to his feet again and took it from her reluctant
fingers, turning it slowly around.

'Be careful, won't you!' It was like parting with something infinitely precious and she didn't care for his abrupt
handling of it.

For once he didn't appear to hear her. His thick, dark
brows were meeting over considering eyes in a frown of
surprised concentration, and Petra, staring at him, felt a
sudden agony that had nothing to do with her immediate
circumstances. Yet why should she feel so antagonistic
when he was merely looking at it? 'Please,' she gasped,
unable to help herself, as if he was desecrating something
wholly dear to her, 'please give it back.'

He took no immediate notice, except that his glance
flicked curiously to her anxious young face. 'Don't worry,'
he said calmly, 'I'm not about to destroy your undoubted
proof, if that's what you're afraid of. It's really quite remarkable.' His finger lightly touched the faint scrawl in the
bottom right-hand corner. 'The same artist, even. He must
have done two. Needless to say, I'm impressed.'

Uncertainly Petra stared up into his face. 'My records
quote two—one for our ancestor to bring over here. He
must have looked after it well.'

'Yes,' Neil Cameron's mouth smiled, 'he must have been
a man of some vanity. I believe I resemble him. Was it
somewhat disconcerting to meet him in the flesh and find
you disliked him, especially when you have obviously such
a high regard for the man in the painting?'

'No!' Confusion swam as Neil Cameron deviously
pounced on what bewildered her. Hastily she restrained her
twitching fingers which seemed to be groping blindly towards it. 'I mean, I like the portrait and—and I have no
reason to dislike you.'

'I hope not.' Perplexingly his voice contained an unwelcome threat. 'A few careless strokes can devastate a picture, Petronella, but not me!'

Meeting his darkly enigmatical gaze, Petra shivered, feeling the ground, in some peculiar fashion, giving way under her feet. For the first time since entering this house she felt something like real apprehension moving inside her and, because the Cameron in the portrait didn't watch her so unkindly, her eyes went back to him as words eluded her.

Her eyes riveted on it so eloquently that Neil Cameron grinned maliciously, 'So much wasted emotion! Why not transfer some of it to where it might be better appreciated? My grandfather used to say I resembled the first emigrating Cameron more than I realised.'

She flushed, glancing at his broad-shouldered, strongly muscled frame. 'I can see you look rather like him,' she allowed cautiously.

He stared again at the portrait and nodded his tall head. 'I have been said to share some of his ruthless characteristics, but that you must judge for yourself.' He laid the picture carefully then on a side table. 'Leave it,' he admonished, when she would have picked it up. 'Tomorrow is soon enough to decide what's to be done with it.'

And with you! His smooth voice seemed full of words left unsaid, explicit warnings, making Petra again reluctantly aware that she had a certain role to play, one which certainly couldn't include fighting him.

'Of course,' she murmured, deceptively submissive.

'The cousin angle,' he mused, 'can scarcely come into it after all this time. I guess it would be almost impossible to define, but if it pleases you, we can leave it.'

'Does this mean we can stay a—a little while?'

'If you like.'

Not much encouragement there. He appeared amused by her shortage of breath. 'I would be very grateful,' she confessed over-elaborately.

'Would you?' His eyes lingered on her more hopeful face in which relief was more clearly displayed than she knew. 'You're a very attractive girl, Petronella. I might be perfectly willing to go along with any relationship you care to name.'

On the face of it that sounded extremely congenial, too congenial, maybe, but could she afford to examine too closely every suave inflection in his mocking voice? His co-operation might be short-lived, she suspected, should she try to make their stay here permanent. It was only when she thought of David that her resolve strengthened instead of weakening.

'You came over by plane?' He sat down facing her again and his light query interrupted her pensive thoughts.

'Yes.' Her reply was brief, necessarily guarded. She didn't want him asking all sorts of questions about that, and, with his astute mind, reading all she left unsaid between the lines.

'When did you arrive in this country?'

'Some time ago.' It had been merely two days, but she needn't elaborate. The last two days had seemed more like that number of years!

'Where else have you been?' Neil Cameron stretched back lazily, as if just getting into his stride, his whole demeanour expressing a slightly satirical interest.

Her full, pink mouth compressed. 'Oh, around. Calgary.'

His eyes crinkled, although with suspicion or amusement she couldn't be sure. 'You aren't particularly forthcoming.'

She forced a charming rueful smile. 'I'm sorry if I'm not being very entertaining, but I am feeling rather tired. I must confess it's all been a bit more than I'd expected.' Which happened to be nothing less than the truth!

'It's not always easy to find your way around by car,' he agreed. 'You could have done better to have travelled by rail. Canada has an extremely impressive network of railways.'

'That car!' He had made her think of it again. 'Will it be awfully expensive to hang on to?'

'Didn't you enquire, Petronella?'

Petra flushed, wishing she hadn't mentioned it. She hadn't meant to! 'I didn't anticipate damaging it,' she hedged.

'I'll have a mechanic look over it tomorrow,' he promised, readily enough. 'If he can fix it, it could be wiser to return it to the firm you hired it from. They usually have branches all over.'

'Yes,' she murmured, somewhat bleakly, wondering why she had ever hired it in the first place, where she would find the money to settle up. It would take her last penny— dollar, she corrected herself silently, with a mirthless smile. 'There's such a lot I hadn't thought of,' she shrugged unhappily. 'I think the strain of finding my way around and having David to look after ...'

'He's not your responsibility, surely?'

'We're orphans.' She hadn't intended he should know so soon, nor that she should sound so bereft when she did tell him but it could be better this way.

Although Neil Cameron voiced no immediate regret he took it exactly as she had hoped he would. 'So this trip was really to help your brother over such a loss?'

'In a way.'

She thought his expression a little kinder. 'It's a bit rough on you, isn't it? A boy like David needs a man's hand.'

'Oh, no!' Her protective instincts rebelled before his harder tones. 'That is,' she agreed nervously, 'I suppose you're partly right, but he isn't too strong. He needs a lot of sympathetic understanding.'

'Merely a woman's point of view,' he said curtly. 'Too much of that could retard his growth.'

'You wouldn't understand because you wouldn't need it,' Petra flared, quite unable to see Neil Cameron as delicate at any stage of his life. He was too much of a man, too immensely arrogant, with all the assurance which went with it.

'I was never coddled, Petronella, if that's what you're getting at. Nor am I now. Unless,' he added wickedly, 'you intend looking after me as well?'

Suddenly apprehensive, Petra stared at him, remembering something which had bothered her all evening. 'I'm sorry, I should have asked if you're married. Or do you live alone?' The information she had stated that he had no wife, but she could scarcely confess how closely she had looked into his affairs. And, of course, her information could be wrong?

'I thought I heard you mention this before?' he drawled.

'No—I don't think so.'

'I have a stepmother and half-sister,' his deep blue eyes held Petra's sardonically, 'both of whom are away at present, being altogether more addicted to city life than to that of the wild, open prairie. Occasionally they do honour me with a visit. But no, I don't have a wife. Which isn't to say I couldn't do with one, Petronella. When a man has a ranch this size to run she could be a help.'

A help? Would he really only regard his wife in this light? A kind of business proposition? 'You sound very cool about it,' she retorted, startled.

'Better be that way and choose wisely than to allow my emotions to tempt me beyond my better judgment,' he smiled. 'I also have my sons to think of.'

'Your sons?'

'Oh, I haven't any yet,' he said softly, 'but I intend to.'

Really, he had a nerve! He might just as well consult a computer. Or could it be his way of letting her know he would never consider a silly little English girl fit for such a star-spangled job? Well, she certainly wouldn't be applying for it! All she wanted was to assure David's future, that he at least had a start in life. A few more years wouldn't hurt Neil Cameron. If he had waited this long he couldn't be in any hurry to find this paragon he required as a wife! 'I see,' she shrugged, non-committally.

'Thank you, Petronella,' he returned, equally polite.

Because his cynicism didn't match up to her Cameron of the portrait she jumped to her feet. Frightened he could guess what she was thinking, she said quickly, 'I'm sorry I won't be able to meet your stepmother and sister. Perhaps another time.'

He nodded affably as he came up beside her. 'I should

like them to see all this fair hair.' His hand went out, out-rageously, to touch the silky flow of it. 'You obviously don't take after the dark Camerons.'

'My mother,' she gasped, as the lingering pressure of his fingers caused a strange quiver, 'was Italian and very fair.'

'Which accounts for a lot,' he rejoined coolly, if his exact meaning was far from clear. 'I imagine you must have been an entrancing *bambina*.'

'Perhaps.' She tried desperately to hang on to her equi-librium, to affect his cool sophistication. Surely he wasn't going to start pawing her, like all those other men?

'Something wrong, Petronella? You have the appearance of a young girl about to be ravished. Shouldn't you worry about this before you step into the dens of big bad men?'

Her laughter was a little too shrill as she jerked away from him. 'I think you enjoy teasing me, Mr Cameron!'

'Neil,' he commanded. 'Surely, if we're to be cousins?'

'Yes, Neil ...' She forced herself to remember she might just have two days to impress him as to the desirability of this and that she would never manage it if she continued to act like a naïve little fool. 'I think I'm tired,' she glanced up at him slowly, making her long curling lashes flutter im-pressively. 'Would you mind if I went to bed?'

He towered over her, giving her the impression she was very small and fragile, something which, if he so wished, he might crush. 'A retreat?' he quirked, mildly sarcastic. 'It can't be the Scottish blood in you, surely? Maybe mine hasn't been so diluted by charming infiltration. I always advance.'

'Not on helpless friends, I hope?' she replied nimbly, yet feeling a fine flare of fright that turned her towards the door.

'Don't be too sure of that!' he laughed, his eyes con-taining, in spite of his growling laughter, more than a hint of derisive speculation. 'Goodnight, Petronella, sleep well. We still have things to discuss, but nothing that can't wait until morning.'

That night Petra's dreams were disturbed many times by

the black shadow of a menacing Cameron and she woke repeatedly, bathed in perspiration, seeing his face looming above her like some ghostly threat. To add to this her wrist still hurt whenever she turned over in bed, and eventually she decided to get up and dress. The light of a new day glowed outside with the promise of heat to come, so she discarded her jeans in favour of a skirt and thin body shirt. Beneath the skirt, apart from a pair of brief panties, her long slender legs were bare as she declined on such a fine morning to wear tights, while her top clung to her enticing young figure like a second skin.

Looking in on David, to see if he wanted to accompany her on a short half hour's exploration, she found him still sleeping. He must have been tired out, and, as it was still only seven, she thought it better to let him stay where he was. After tucking in the blanket which was trailing on the floor she pushed the fair hair gently back from off his hot forehead before leaving him.

Swiftly, making no sound, she ran downstairs and out the front door on to the soft grass. Still holding her worn sandals in her hand, she let the morning fresh dew soak her bare feet, exulting unconsciously in the pagan feel of it as she walked. Not having walked like this since she had left Redwell, the memory brought the dampness of nostalgic tears to her eyes.

Cautiously she sought her way around. She dared not go far on two counts. First she was frightened David would wake and be alarmed if he found her gone. Secondly she didn't want to get lost. Everything seemed so vast that she had little doubt it could happen, and being naturally adventurous she might easily find herself in another awkward situation. Yesterday's experience was something she wouldn't forget in a hurry, and while Neil seemed disposed to overlook it, it might not do to try his patience too far, no matter whose fault it might be. If she wasn't careful she might bump into his dictatorial foreman and, somehow, on such a beautiful morning she didn't feel like another nerve-racking encounter!

Pausing beside a white-railed fence some way from the

house, she gazed around. The size of the property looked immense. The house, from where she stood, huge and sprawling, and behind it, through the trees, cabins and stockyards covered acres of ground. At least, to Petra's startled eyes, they appeared to, and over all the Rockies rose, majestically invulnerable, shadowing the foothills. Their peaks she could follow to the sky, the lower ones clad in green forest but the higher ones bleak and bare, impressive while as intimidating as Neil Cameron himself!

Petra felt a dry shiver run right over her, even as the brilliant sunshine grew warmer. For so long she had known Neil Cameron's face, but to meet him in person had seemed to shatter all her preconceived illusions. He was altogether a more formidable figure than she had ever imagined and it seemed hopeless to try and convince herself he was not the same person as that in the portrait. Before arriving here she had vowed dramatically that she would be willing to sacrifice even herself in order to help David, but she realised now this had only been an idea she had liked to play with. Under all her wilder suppositions she had been convinced of a father figure, lonely and frail, willing and even eager to welcome a new daughter. Neil Cameron, in the flesh, had devastated such unworldly dreaming and shown her what a flagrant coward she really was!

Yet now, without money, her options had gone absolutely and she was aware, with a sinking heart, that there was only one way to enslave a man like Cameron. Only one way, if she could manage it, to get what she wanted!

Pushing this—another act of weakness, to the back of her mind, she decided to try and find her unfortunate car. This might help to take her thoughts off her lack of courage and her aching wrist. Maybe, she pondered, on a more optimistic note, Cameron's stepmother might happen to turn up and save her? Then despondently she thrust such wistful hopes aside. Other women rarely seemed very kindly disposed towards girls who managed to find themselves in her position, Mrs Cameron was unlikely to prove the exception!

There was no one about. Maybe Neil Cameron had been called away or hadn't yet left his bed. He probably hadn't retired until the early hours. Last night he had had the look of a man who rarely tired. Petra's wandering footsteps took her in the direction of a large shed, where the sound of muted hammering came to her ears. To her utter surprise the shed contained not only a helicopter but a small, expensive-looking plane, and, at the very end of this impressive evidence of Cameron's affluence, her car. Going closer, she could see a man, a young man, crouched beside it with a pile of wrenches behind him.

'Excuse me.' Slightly breathless, she hobbled towards him, impatient that she had left her shoes on the grass and forgotten about them. 'Is it going to be all right?'

The young man stumbled to his feet, appearing both startled and sheepish to find Petra standing over him. 'I'm sorry, ma'am. Did you want something?'

Petra smiled at him because he seemed a pleasant young man. 'I only asked if you could mend it.'

'Yes, ma'am,' this time he grinned in a friendly manner, 'I think so. In fact if it belongs to you, I'll guarantee it, but I've only been working on it a couple of hours.'

'Two hours? But it's barely seven now!'

'Sure, ma'am,' the boy's eyes, taking in her fair hair and slim figure, grew warmer, 'we rise early.'

'Oh, I see.' She drew back a little from the boy's rather obvious admiration, her defence mechanism, as always these days, too ready to object. 'I wonder——' she began, her smile warily fading.

It disappeared altogether to find a proprietorial hand descending on her shoulder from behind and Neil Cameron's cool voice in her ear. 'You should be helping, not hindering, Petronella!'

Hastily she turned, in doing so bumping right up against him and feeling absolutely covered in confusion beneath his smouldering blue gaze. Why should he look so annoyed? When, unable to sustain his ice-bound glance, her thick lashes dropped, she felt even worse as her eyes encountered his brown chest through the half-open front of his checked shirt. It was broad and bare and covered with fine, dark hair, the shocking maleness of it filling her with an alarming repulsion which must have shown in her eyes.

'I've only just come,' she choked, wondering why, when she felt such abhorrence, her heart should be beating so furiously. 'I was merely asking about the extent of the damage. Surely it would seem unnatural not to?'

His eyes glittered slightly as hers remained, as if in fascinated horror, on his chest. He ignored her resentful query as if he hadn't heard it and waved the young man back to his job. 'You seem rather too distraught to make sense,' he mocked. 'Have you had breakfast? You look as though you'd spent the last hour running through the dew.'

'No, not yet.' She was conscious that his steady gaze unnerved her. When he looked at her, she thought crossly, her breath still uneven, it was as if he was weighing up all her assets, but completely impassively, almost as he might study one of his priceless steers. But then he was probably used to a different kind of reaction from his woman friends. Possible antagonism, such as hers, didn't interest him.

'Come with me,' he ordered, as if her fragile uncertainties didn't hold his attention. 'You look as if you could do with a little feeding up. Right now I think I could crush you very easily, and if you keep on looking at me as you are doing, cousin or no cousin, I might be tempted to demonstrate.'

Giving her no other option but to follow, he grasped her slender white arm and led her away. Petra, casting a glance of hidden anguish towards the small red car and the now industrious mechanic, decided not to struggle. Opposition, she sensed, was what men like Neil Cameron throve on, and she appeared to have displeased him enough this morning without chancing her luck any further.

Yet his grip on her arm was so tight as to actually hurt her and forced her, before they reached the house, to voice another half-strangled protest. 'I only asked if he could mend it, nothing else!'

'Quite, Petronella.' He didn't ease his long strides. 'Didn't I tell you last night your car would be taken care of? You would only distract a man by hovering around him. What had you in mind? The passing of an encouraging smile with every wrench?'

'Don't be silly!' Hot indignation rose, but while she longed to express her resentment in a stronger fashion she had sense enough not to. There was too much at stake. 'I can't be wrong every time,' she said instead. 'I was only trying to help!'

'You can do that best by keeping out of the way.' He paused outside the screen door at the back of the house, turning his dark head to study her consideringly again. 'You're extremely decorative, little cousin, if this accounts for the degree of protectiveness I can't recall feeling before. It almost convinces me there must be a blood tie between us, however slight, to produce such a sensation of having known you for a long time. An affinity if you like, but one you don't necessarily have to share with others.'

Momentarily, as she stared up at him, her expression was completely unguarded. 'I feel it too.'

'But you've had my likeness, remember,' he pointed out, reasonably enough. 'I've had no such painting of you, yet you seem wholly familiar. Perhaps in a few years' time, if you come back again, we might enjoy an even better relationship.'

'Yes,' she agreed, while having no clear idea just what he was getting at. It was a strange remark to make, one she instinctively distrusted, but it might simply be a hint that he wasn't interested if she sought to prolong her stay. As she had already guessed this it was nothing new!

In a way she was becoming accustomed to, he gave her no time to meditate but swept her inside, into a huge kitchen where breakfast was set out on a wide, white scrubbed table and large slices of pink ham were sizzling with an extremely appetising smell in an outsize pan. Mrs Allen presided, in a mammoth, floury white apron, in which she was just removing a tray of sourdough biscuits from the oven.

Instantly, in this big kitchen, Petra felt at home. It was like being a child again at Redwell and she smiled at Mrs Allen as the woman came to serve her after she had sat down. Neil Cameron, it seemed, had already had one breakfast but, as this had been hours ago, was quite ready to eat another.

Petra, while beseeching Mrs Allen not to overload her plate, remembered David. 'Would you mind,' she asked Neil quickly, 'if I go and get him?'

He glanced at her idly as he pulled out his own chair and reached for the coffee pot. 'I think I can hear someone coming now. It can only be him.'

Seconds later, a scrubbed-looking David entered the room and, after wishing them all a polite good morning, slid into the seat Mrs Allen indicated beside Petra. 'You should have woken me up,' he reproached her, in stiff undertones.

'I thought you were in need of the extra rest,' Petra fussed. 'You were tired.'

'You always think I'm tired,' he retorted, his thin face mutinous, 'but we're not in London now!'

'Last night you couldn't stay awake.'

'I'm all right this morning. You should have ...'

At this juncture, just as Petra began to look anxiously helpless, Neil chose to intervene. His eyes fixed keenly on David's hot face. 'There's no hurry. I guess it's still reasonably early by anyone's standards. I'm taking your sister into town after breakfast, David, to let the doc see her arm. Would you like to come?'

'I'm not sure.' David looked back at Neil intently, then appeared to draw a deep breath. 'I'd rather stay here, sir, if you don't mind. That is, if you'll promise to look after Petra?'

'Oh, I'll do that,' Cameron agreed solemnly. 'It will be a change for you not to have her on your mind.'

'Well, it's only men she's scared of,' David explained before Petra could restrain him.

'You're making it up!' Trying to avoid Neil's glance of studied interest, she almost glared at her brother, as if willing him to take it back. 'David imagines a lot of things,' she said, to no one in particular.

Neil ignored her as he turned, man to man, to David. 'Just as long as you stay around the house, you won't come to any harm. After lunch I'll take you around myself, but until then I'd advise you not to go too far.'

As David nodded, obviously with Neil, prepared to be reasonable, Petra took a deep breath. This and more she might need to defy Cameron. 'I don't want to go to town this morning. My arm feels much better.' It didn't really feel that good, but she had no money to spare for doctor's bills.

Neil pinned her with a steely, no-nonsense gaze. 'Don't argue, there's a good girl. I'm responsible for your accident, or rather my steer was, which amounts to the same thing.'

'Petra can't afford it,' David offered absently, being wholly occupied with spreading jam on his flapjacks.

'Don't be silly!' Petra viewed his continued indiscretion with growing despair. Didn't he remember anything she had told him? The flare of colour in her cheeks made her utter too emphatically, 'Of course I can. In fact I'll insist!'

'But . . .? Oh, I'm sorry.' David's muttered apology, after glancing up at Petra's pink face, only made it sound worse, but to her relief Neil, thoughtfully stirring sugar into his coffee, didn't appear to have heard.

'Do you have a jacket, Petronella?' he asked, lifting his thick, rather feminine lashes, to let his eyes frown over her.

'Yes,' she said quickly, deciding suddenly it might be wiser not to protest any more. There couldn't be much wrong with her wrist, surely, or she wouldn't have been able to bear it, and if he was prepared to waste time taking her all the way to town—well, this was up to him. And it was perhaps better that David wasn't going with them as she was beginning to wonder what he was about to come out with next. She must do her best to keep the two of them apart until she had another talk with David.

Neil was on his feet. 'Run along and fetch it, then,' he commanded, as she made no move. 'I'd like to get away as soon as possible. Meet me outside. I just want a quick word with my foreman.'

Halfway out of her chair Petra stopped. 'Your fore-man?'

'That's what I said, Petronella.'

She ignored his dryness, to say eagerly, 'I wonder if I might come with you—to see him, I mean. I feel I ought to thank him properly for his help last night.'

'Now that would really be something,' Cameron drawled, 'but don't let it bother you—that wasn't my foreman.'

'No!'

'No, Petronella. I'm afraid you might not see that particular man again. If it helps, I can assure you, he was quite satisfied with what he'd already received.'

Which was about as clear as mud, Petra decided crossly, smiling faintly at Mrs Allen before running upstairs.

CHAPTER FOUR

SOME fifteen minutes later she was sitting beside Neil in the light aircraft, fastening her seat belt before they took off. She felt the jolt in her stomach as they became airborne, the familiar ache of tension she could never dispel, no matter how much she travelled. She glanced sideways, taking in Neil's dark head, his indisputable expertise at the controls and, surprisingly, felt the tightness inside her relax. It was as if some part of her had acknowledged complete confidence in him, something she had never felt before with any other man, except perhaps her father.

She was watching the clouds, oddly content to let the tension drain out of her, and his question startled her. 'Have you done much flying, Petronella?'

'A little,' she nodded cautiously, 'on big aircraft. I'm afraid not many people in England have their own personal planes.'

'You don't have the distances we have here,' deliberately he misunderstood her meaning. 'You have to remember Canada is the second largest country. Even this province of Alberta is around 255,285 square miles, which is more than the whole of Great Britain.'

'I realise,' she retorted dryly, 'this could account for it.'

'It's a geographical fact,' he grinned. 'You don't have to resent it.'

'But it's a fact which allows you to develop and grow rich.'

His eyebrow quirked. 'To come here I guess our mutual ancestor forsook all his home comforts and I doubt if he ever replaced them in his lifetime. To some extent we're still a pioneer country, Petronella, but there's reward enough for those prepared to work for it.'

Always, Petronella thought mutinously, Neil Cameron seemed able to set her down a peg or two! To argue with this man was like tangling with a brick wall of logic. 'You have more than one aircraft,' she pointed out. 'Do you use both for merely coming to town?'

'No,' his lean, powerful frame twisted to glance down at the passing country, 'we use them a lot to search out cattle in the scrub, which saves plenty of valuable time. They have other uses, too, such as when we want to visit a neighbour, either on business or social matters. A hundred miles in a plane can be nothing, but on second-class roads in a car it can waste a whole day.'

Neil Cameron would naturally have a social life, Petra pondered, a slight frown marking her smooth brow, which he misinterpreted.

'Relax,' he ordered, his glance flicking over her, noticing, no doubt, the cheap cut of her apparel. She was wearing her jacket, but it was hot. 'I'm glad you haven't discarded your sandals again,' he approved. He didn't add that he thought them shabby and she hoped this had escaped him.

'You've been around, I take it?' he asked conversationally.

'Oh, yes,' she said brightly, not mentioning that during the past year she had been nowhere.

'I should have expected a girl with your looks to be married.' He gave her another comprehensive appraisal. 'How come you've escaped?'

She retorted sharply, her pulse suddenly agitated, 'I could ask you the same thing. Myself, I don't want to be married.'

'You might change your mind,' his voice taunted. 'No boy-friends?'

'No.'

'If you were older, Petronella,' he drawled, 'I should judge that you'd had a disastrous love affair.'

'Why should you think that?'

'The way you almost shrink every time I get near you, and David did remark that you were scared of men.'

So he had heard. She might have known! 'I've only known you since yesterday.'

'No explanation. Not so far as you and I are concerned.'

'Does there have to be one?' Why had she placed herself in such a humiliating situation?

'Yes, I think so, but I don't want to have to drag it out of you, Petronella. Be our acquaintance brief or not, if we were in the helicopter I would put down right now and guarantee before many minutes you would be confessing all. If you didn't approve of my methods, I would almost guarantee you enjoyed them. I don't consider you too young for a lot of things, Petronella, especially with your kind of mouth.'

Flushing scarlet, Petra stared down at her hands, the full, curved mouth he so admired compressed. The insolence of the man! Obviously, with his arrogant good looks, his money and degree of sophistication, he was used to women finding him irresistible. She could even feel her own heart beating wildly, at the thought of all he implied, but this wasn't to say she was ready to be wholly taken over!

With determination she kept her eyes averted from his, pretending to concentrate on the country over which they were passing, but her impression of wild foothills and even wilder-looking prairie, with its scattering of grazing cattle, didn't seem to inspire her. It only increased a sense of pure isolation which, while in itself not frightening, did leave her in little doubt as to the complete vulnerableness of her position. It was enough somehow to convince her that Neil Cameron didn't always threaten idly, and she would be wiser to co-operate, if only to alleviate some of his suspicions. 'I don't happen to care for men very much, on the whole.' In case this didn't sound reasonable, she stammered, 'Of course this doesn't apply to you.'

'I'm gratified.' His voice flicked a little. 'I take it you've had an unhappy experience?'

'No.' Her eyes widened as she realised what he meant. 'At least, not the kind I think you have in mind.'

'I wonder?' He held her confused glance, his eyes slightly narrowed. 'Women have long mastered the art of appearing fragilely innocent. Until a certain point in their relationship it can only leave a man guessing.'

'Yet men are to be admired for their very lack of innocence?' she challenged sarcastically, stung by his egotism.

The plane rose on a current of warm air and he controlled it expertly, as he might a woman. 'That's another of
women's little grievances, isn't it? They don't want an
affair with a man who doesn't entirely know what he's
doing, but they wholly resent the experience he brings with
him.'

'Why shouldn't they?' she asked, but trying to match his
sophistication her voice choked.

'If it adds to their pleasure?'

'Oh ...' Her cheeks crimson again, Petra lowered her
eyes from the dark fascination of his. Why was he talking
to her this way? Almost as if he was making love to her
through the medium of a normal conversation. Yet he
sounded so matter-of-fact as to make her rather prim indignation seem artificial. The way her pulse rate was accelerating left her in doubt that some part of her, at least, was
wholly willing and able to respond! At the same time she
felt it would be indelicate, if not downright beyond her,
to admit it. 'I think we're talking on two different levels,'
she murmured at last.

'The road usually goes up and down to begin with, Petronella,' he teased. 'I'm sure there's a spot where we shall
meet. I might even say I'm looking forward to it. Perhaps
when you come back again.'

Quickly suspicious, she glanced at his lightly mocking
face, on which the strong lines of his profile gave nothing
away. So he was only teasing her, while she had been too
busy jumping to the wrong conclusions? Not that he could
be blamed altogether, she admitted unhappily. Her story
was thin, even to her own ears, and Neil wasn't a man to
swallow everything completely. When he talked so glibly
of her returning was it because he had already concluded
she had no intention of going away? Not if she could help
it—no matter how high a price she was asked to pay! If he
was a man fully aware of women and their needs this could
only mean he would be that much easier to encourage.

To this end she even managed to force some light laughter. 'I'm your cousin, Neil, remember!'

He answered in the same vein, 'It does add a touch of respectability.'

They touched down in Calgary, the chief city of southern Alberta, home of the famous rodeo. A busy city, it was situated in the valley of the Bow river, a tributary of the South Saskatchewan.

'We could have gone to other places, Lethbridge or Medicine Hat,' Neil said, 'but I know a guy here who's a particular wizard with bones. He also finds it convenient to see you this morning, which might not be the case elsewhere.'

Two hours later or thereabouts, they were on their way back. The speed of the whole operation had bewildered Petra and she could scarcely believe it when they were once again boarding the plane. The hospital to which Neil had taken her was cool and white and very efficient, and she had a horrible suspicion that the treatment she had received was the best and most expensive. She had felt it a terrible blow to her pride that she had been unable even to offer to pay. She had felt so awful about it that she hadn't been able to look at Neil and afterwards, outside, she felt she had only made things worse by mumbling ineffectually about settling up.

'You'll do that later,' he had assured her, and though far from happy at his deliberate tones she was forced to leave it at that.

Her arm, fortunately, had not been broken, only sprained at the wrist with a bone slightly out of place. It was now wrapped professionally in fresh bandages. The doctor, apparently an old friend of Neil's from university days, had told her it would be fine in a few days, but advised her not to drive. 'It would only do untold harm,' he had said.

They were almost home before Neil seemed prepared to comment on it. With the delicate cruelty with which she was beginning to associate him, he glanced at her. 'You'll have to prolong your visit now, won't you? Unless you're prepared to travel by train or coach.'

Dismally, Petra glanced away from him. He didn't look as if he meant to be sarcastic, but she recognised that he was taunting her a little. Maybe he guessed she didn't want to leave right away and wasn't sure what to make of it? Again she wondered what his final reactions would be, when she told him she didn't intend leaving, ever.

'I'd rather stay with you, if you don't mind,' she said at last, inadvertently giving the impression that she had been considering.

'You're very welcome, of course,' he replied coolly. 'I think I'd better point out, though, that we're rather busy just now on the ranch, so I won't have a great deal of time to entertain you.'

'No, of course not,' she agreed eagerly, maybe too eagerly judging from the keen glance he shot her. 'I mean,' she hastened, 'I realise you must have a lot to do, but I expect you'll be at home during the evening?'

'You look forward to that?'

'Well,' she hesitated, again cautious as to his exact tones, 'I would like to get to know you properly.'

'Oh, you'll do that, Petronella,' he laughed, but on a thread of seriousness he added emphatically, 'Never doubt it!'

That evening Petra decided to wear her only dress for dinner. She hoped that if Neil saw her in something different he would decide she had an extensive wardrobe and this impression might remain. Men didn't usually notice all that much and if Neil was extra busy, as he had said, he would probably never give her clothes a second thought. She brushed her hair well and left it loose about her shoulders, knowing enough about men to realise they liked the shining fairness of it. While not being over-impressed with it herself, she wondered if it might distract Neil's attention from the too obvious dowdiness of her insignificant grey dress, which might, she thought despairingly, have been more suited to an elderly matron.

Neil, to her relief, seemed quite satisfied to see only her hair and face, which he appeared to study from time to time with a quite definite appreciation. His own clothes, she noticed, were of impeccable cut and, for all his size, he always managed to look supremely elegant. It was this, combined with the impression of latent strength, that Petra found disconcerting, if not a little frightening! She did not want to admit that there could be a lot more to Neil Cameron than she had anticipated. An aura of power moved about him, a sense of absolute maleness and authority, which she supposed might come from long years of handling a huge property like this one. He looked, if one caught him objectively, about as hard and unyielding as the high Rockies which towered above his home. All that devastating formidability could only have grown from the roots of some Celtic ancestry on which had been grafted, over the years, the additional qualities of good Canadian stock. From the one or two remarks he had passed it seemed that for the most part of the year he lived alone, yet he didn't strike her as a man who would be over-fond of his own company. There was a hint of awareness in his eyes on occasion, when he glanced at her, as if a woman might, if only occasionally, interest him. It was there, in that keenly penetrating blueness, and his mouth, which was curving and sensuous, for all the tight hold he kept on it. It was the vertical line between his brows, speaking of some impatience and intolerance, which made Petra doubt suddenly and apprehensively if the softer, more approachable side of him was ever allowed to prevail.

David, who had gone to bed early again, after being allowed to join them for dinner, seemed to share none of her doubts. He had been gone so long with Neil that afternoon that she had only managed a hasty word with him afterwards. Surprisingly, because it had been so long since he had shown enthusiasm over anything, his admiration had bubbled over.

'Neil's super, Petra,' he had said, leaving Petra curiously speechless.

'Just as long as you remember he might not be so nice when I ask if we can stay,' she had muttered, being forced, by lack of time, to leave it at that.

After dinner Neil, as she had feared, began to ask about her life in England.

'Do you have a job to go back to, Petronella?' he enquired.

Petra, who had been bracing herself for something like this, started all the same. 'No,' for a moment she could barely hide the panic in her eyes when she thought of it, 'I did have one but gave it up—to come here.'

'No understanding employer?'

'I can easily find more work,' she said evasively.

'You're trained for something, of course?'

'Nothing specific, if that's what you mean.'

To her relief he didn't, after one faintly contemplative pause, press the issue. Instead he asked agreeably, 'Does David attend a special school?'

'Special . . .?'

'Boarding school, I mean?' he supplied curtly.

'No.' She felt rather flustered by his tone and glanced at him uncertainly. 'He's not very strong, you see.'

'He looks all right to me.'

She wished he would look elsewhere but her face. It would be much easier to evade direct answers if he wasn't staring at her with those penetrating blue eyes! 'That's only because you see him as he is today. He's usually tired out and—and——' her voice trailed off helplessly and she was aghast to find almost a sob in her throat.

That he must have noticed but chose to ignore it was in itself disquieting. Again he didn't persist, but her slight feeling of gratitude died as he passed on to something worse, with what she considered a ruthless disregard for any delicateness of feelings.

'What did your father do?'

'He was a well-known financier.'

'So he was able to leave you well provided for.'

How did she answer this one without giving everything away? 'We've managed,' she replied at least.

He considered this, his eyes still unnerving on her taut face. 'David must sometimes be almost more than you can cope with?'

This could mean many things, but she decided to take it at its face value. 'He's usually very good, no trouble. I worry sometimes, as can be expected,' she added, swiftly dismayed to find she had been on the brink of disclosing some of her worst troubles.

'Naturally,' Neil said mildly. 'David, I think, should go to a good boarding school. I'd say he was more than ready for one. If he began in the fall it would give you a chance to get on with your own life.'

As he rose to pour himself a drink, Petra found herself watching him in rather a dazed fashion. No one knew better than she that David longed to go to boarding school. He might have been there before their father died, but Charles Sinclair had always said twelve was quite soon enough. Petra had suspected her father hadn't wanted to part with him, not because David hadn't wanted to go. Now he would never go. Not unless Neil could be persuaded to send him. This she must ask of him eventually, but she couldn't, yet. Not until she knew him at least a little better. There could be a right way to approach him. He had been kind to David, after a late lunch, showing him around himself. When he had discovered the boy could ride he had mounted him on a smart little palomino pony and taken him off into the foothills.

About this Petra had been a trifle disconcerted, well aware that he could easily have taken them both by truck. She had been unable to accompany them on horseback, because of her bad wrist, and it seemed to her that Neil, knowing this, had deliberately contrived to leave her behind. Her nerves had stretched almost to breaking point during the remainder of the afternoon while she had wondered how many, and what sort of questions he was asking her brother. When David returned she had been ashamed to learn that he had asked nothing, but she still couldn't rid herself of the feeling that he had planned it with every in-

tention of robbing her, if only temporarily, of some peace
of mind.

'My own life isn't of great importance,' she said, her
voice strained but indifferent as Neil returned to his seat
and obviously awaited her comment.

'It could be,' his eyes considered her wide grey ones, 'if
not to you, then someone else.'

She supposed he was talking of David, so was startled
predictably, when he added suavely, 'A lot of women
would give everything they possessed to look like you.
Beauty, Petronella, is not to be scorned. It's a highly sale-
able commodity, as you might one day discover.'

'Why, that's—that's a beastly thing to say!' Highly in-
flammable, she jumped to her feet. Somehow she couldn't
seem to bear his hurtful amusement, especially when it
happened to be too near the mark for total comfort. Non-
plussed, she halted, at the beginning of wild flight. 'I'm
sorry,' she muttered, a world of desolation suddenly clouding her clear young voice, 'I think I'm too tired to realise
what I'm saying. If you'll excuse me, I would like to go upstairs. I know you were only teasing.'

He was beside her, very dark and tall, his hand, far from
cousin-like, upon her trembling shoulder. 'I think neither
of us can be too sure of that, Petronella,' he mocked, his
gaze lancing through her. When she didn't reply, because
she somehow could not, he turned her almost gently towards the staircase, standing watching her like some contemplative bird of prey as she stumbled unsteadily upwards, away from him.

Petra felt secretly ashamed during the next few days that
she must pretend her wrist was worse than it actually was.
It was painful at times, but the tablets she had been given
helped and she knew she didn't have to make such a fuss
about it as she did. She didn't say much, but she became
curiously addicted to appearing helpless when Neil was
around and seeing his immediate solicitude as he studied
her pale face. Not that she was so very pale anymore. She
was quickly acquiring a soft golden tan that went beautifully with her silky fair hair, and her figure, with all the

good food, was filling out a little and rounding. While she didn't put on much weight, the extra pound or two was definitely attractive.

David, too, looked better, and had quickly settled down. It should have made Petra feel happier, but contrarily did not that all David now seemed bent on was staying here. It was amazing, if something not to be taken too seriously, the liking he seemed to be developing for the country. He was out and about all day, either with Neil or the cowboys on the ranch, and seemed to lose all inclination to spend much time with Petra. Fervently, in private, he begged Petra that they should stay.

'It's really nice here,' he exclaimed. 'But if Neil can't do with us you could perhaps get a job in one of the towns. Wouldn't it be just the same as working in England? Couldn't we emigrate sort of officially? I'd much rather not go back to London again.'

When David pleaded like this, so innocently, she found it difficult to remind him that the future could be very bleak for both of them if Neil refused to help.

Daily she was getting to know Neil better, if sometimes she felt she knew him not at all. Each evening, after dinner, they talked, although occasionally he went to his study and worked. It was only then that Petra ever felt lonely, when he cut himself off from her abruptly and the door closed behind him. She found herself looking forward to his company more and more, as she gained confidence from it. Unconsciously, when she let herself imagine he really was her Cameron of the painting, she grew enchanted. But this was when he was in a good mood. When he changed, as he sometimes did, and the ruthless sharpness of his tongue hurt, then he became a stranger, and one she knew she would do well to be wary of. This was what, she was convinced, made her pulse race and her legs feel often unsteady when he came unexpectedly near her.

One evening, just before dinner, a visitor arrived. It was windy outside and they hadn't heard the helicopter, nor did they know that anyone was there until the door opened and a young man walked in.

Startled, Petra turned her fair head to stare at him. He wasn't as tall as Cameron or as well built, but altogether he seemed a very presentable young man with a rather pleasant, open face. Somewhere in his middle twenties, Petra guessed.

'Hello, Neil,' he grinned, striding across the room towards him. 'I heard you had a visitor and my curiosity reached the stage of pains in my stomach. I wondered if it would be Mrs Cameron and Janey, maybe with a guest, but Mrs Allen tells me I'm wrong.'

Whether Neil was vexed or pleased by this newcomer's appearance, Petra couldn't guess. There was, as usual, nothing much in his face to indicate which way he was feeling. Laconically he viewed his eagerly smiling visitor. 'Sorry you have to be disappointed,' he drawled rather dryly. 'If you thought it was Janey you certainly didn't hurry,' he added significantly, before effecting introductions.

Oliver Hurd was immediately taken with Petra. 'Your cousin!' His low, boyish whistle of surprise showed appreciation, but was nothing to the frank admiration betrayed by his eyes. He didn't mention Janey again.

'Nothing's certain yet,' Neil cautioned, his eyes sharply amused on Petra's flushed cheeks. 'Petronella, I'm afraid, is more enthusiastic than I. We happen to share an ancestor who came out here nearly two hundred years ago, but this shouldn't discourage us from looking for something somewhere.'

'You don't say!' Oliver still gazed at Petra, as if he very much liked what he saw. 'We heard about your accident and were sorry.'

Neil slanted her a glance. 'You see how news travels, Petronella?'

'Yes,' she laughed, thinking it was just like home. She tried to ignore an inner suspicion that her continued presence here might embarrass Neil in some way.

They talked a while, Oliver asking and Petra answering his questions while Neil drank sparingly and watched them. Oliver took little persuading to stay for dinner but left soon afterwards. Clearly he was entirely charmed with Petra and promised to return soon.

She didn't believe he would, but he did come back twice during the following week, although whether specifically to see her she wasn't sure. She found him agreeable and, because Neil was out so much, he was company, but this was all. He wasn't a man she could ever fall in love with, but at least she didn't feel nervous of him and he was very easy to get on with.

Neil might not hold her responsible for Oliver's visits, but Petra doubted if he altogether approved. Oliver, he told her dryly, was supposed to be in love with his half-sister and both families wanted the match. Janey wanted it very much. Oliver didn't strike her as a man filled with a consuming passion, unless he was good at concealing it. He didn't bother to do much more than nod when Neil told him Janey should be home within the next few weeks, maybe sooner.

On Oliver's next visit Petra was wandering by herself by the creek. 'Don't you swim?' he asked when he found her and viewed her hot face. 'Hasn't Neil taken you to the lake? It's quite warm enough now. It's only earlier in the year that the water can be treacherous. The sun can be hot, but it's like ice beneath the water.'

'Hello!' she smiled, even in her shabby jeans very lovely. Oliver's ability to deliver a lengthy speech in seconds impressed her. 'No, I'm not going in.' She just hadn't the nerve to confess she couldn't, not while pretending her wrist still wasn't strong enough. 'David swims every day, now,' she added quickly. 'I usually sit and watch and I can see he enjoys it.'

'Your kid brother certainly seems to be coming out of his shell.' Oliver climbed down from the truck he had borrowed to come and find her. 'How come you're all alone?' His glance flickered around as if searching for someone else. 'How'd you get here? I can't see your car.'

'No.' She didn't want to think of the little red car, gathering dust in the corner of the huge hangar, nor of the bill that must be steadily mounting for its hire. 'Neil dropped me off. They're busy inoculating some calves which he said were missed in the spring. He promised to pick me up in an hour.' She didn't confess he had asked her to go with him but, because she was finding his presence more and more disturbing, she had refused.

'Good for Neil,' Oliver grumbled good-humouredly as he dropped to the ground beside her. 'Some guys get all the breaks! Actually, Petra, I'm on my way to town and wondered if you'd come with me. If you won't come for my sake there are always the shops. Being a woman you can't possibly resist them!'

Petra gazed at him doubtfully, even apprehensively. It was kind of him to think of her—if kind was the right word. She couldn't help guessing Oliver found her attractive—but his admiration should be kept for Janey. If she went to town with him Neil would probably accuse her of encouraging him. A sigh of regret passed her lips lightly. She didn't doubt she would have enjoyed a trip out with Oliver. She didn't find herself shrinking from him as she did from other men, as she still did sometimes with Neil. But she had to refuse him. He was smartly dressed, for one thing, and she had nothing to match him. Nor any money! 'Some other time, perhaps,' she hedged reluctantly.

'Oh, come on, Petra!' he laughed. 'What's to stop you? It's only for a few hours. I'm not going to kidnap you, no matter how much I'd like to. You even look as if you needed a change. Neil's place can sure match any of your British estates, but that doesn't surely mean you can't go anywhere else?'

'I'd better not, Oliver.' She found it very difficult not to give in when he looked at her so entreatingly.

'You don't like me!' Surprising her, he sounded really unhappy.

'It's not because I don't like you. I do—a lot,' she cried indiscreetly, an unconscious awareness of Neil's disapproval making her reckless. 'Only David's been out all day and when Neil takes me home I must see where he is. I can't expect Mrs Allen to be forever keeping an eye on him.'

For a moment it seemed that Oliver, as if seeing through the thinness of her excuse, was going to argue, but suddenly he subsided. 'Okay, then.' Disappointed, if not too obviously despairing, he agreed ruefully to accept her decision and said he must go. 'I have one of the hands with me,' he explained. 'He has some pressing family business in town and I have to take him. Now I'll have nothing to do but hang around by myself until he's ready to go home.'

'I'm sorry, Oliver.' While uncertain that she could wholly believe in such a woeful aspect, she looked gently up at him, as if seeking a way to soften the blow.

She didn't realise how beautiful she was, her face up-turned like some delicate flower, her eyes thickly fringed and mysterious, like two great shadowed moorland pools. Oliver seemed quite unable to resist what looked so clearly like an invitation. He bent his head and, before she could stop him, pulled her gently into his arms and kissed her lips. Neither of them saw Neil approaching in the distance.

Petra found herself almost gasping with dismay as Oliver at last let her go, as if he was, in reality, rather scared of his own daring. His face flushed as he muttered, 'Goodbye, sweetheart,' and within seconds he was gone, his borrowed truck disappearing in a cloud of dust. Not even then did he notice Neil.

Petra did, though. She was aware of him in the time it took him to grind to a halt. She didn't fail to see, as he stepped out beside her, how his eyes lingered contemptuously on her softly coloured cheeks, her trembling, rose-red mouth.

'Who was that?' he hissed quietly, his eyes almost cutting her in two.

Petra suspected he knew very well! She also recalled, her nerves jumping, everything he had said about Oliver and his sister. 'Oliver,' she stammered helplessly, 'just called to ask if I'd like to go to town.' Oliver's brief kiss had upset her, but Neil's icy demeanour, she found, made her feel much worse.

'Why didn't you?'

'I don't know. At least,' she lowered her eyes, unable

to meet the brilliant coldness of his, 'I might have done, but my clothes are getting a bit tatty, as I didn't bring so many.'

'I'm well aware of the precise state of your wardrobe,' he enlightened her disconcertingly. 'In town you might have had the opportunity to replenish it to some extent.'

Petra realised it was what anyone under normal circumstances would have done. She could only flush unhappily and stare at her toes.

'Oliver might even have bought you a few articles of clothing,' Cameron went on outrageously, utterly daunting her with his taunting grin. 'That outfit you have on is enough to encourage any red-blooded man.'

'It's been washed too many times,' she defended the rather shrunken cotton shirt and pants which clung too revealingly to every taut line of her slim, provocative figure.

'I must see if you can't be persuaded to come shopping with me, Petronella.' His glance, sharply calculating, slid over her again. 'I don't mind what I see myself, but I don't want others enjoying the same privileges.'

She couldn't take him seriously, although his hand cynicism hurt beyond belief. Maybe he was just trying to drive her away. Did he think a few insults would do the trick? Desperately she wished she could afford to slap his handsome, mocking face, but she knew she must listen when every instinct warned her against it. She lifted her head, staring past him towards the tumbling sparkling waters of the creek, knowing only a terrible desolation.

'I think Oliver only meant to be neighbourly,' she said weakly, looking too slender and fragile to be wholly convincing.

Neil seemed to soften a little, if wryly, as if something of her inner conflict got through to him, 'I don't want to quarrel with you, Petronella, especially as you happen to be my guest. I don't particularly want to remind you that I told you Oliver was not to be encouraged.'

So he had seen that too! 'I didn't encourage him,' she

flushed painfully scarlet. 'He did kiss me, I'll admit, but a kiss is nothing!'

'So he didn't make an impression? Or is it that you regard kisses lightly? Two a penny, with little regard of any possible effect.'

'If only I could convince you!' She was moved by a sense of urgency she could put no name to. Neil towered over her and she was suddenly aware, through the open front of his shirt, of the pulse beating strongly over his heart. It seemed to indicate a slightly explosive quality only partly held in check. Fright moved turbulently through her, like a dark summer wind before a storm. 'I don't even like being kissed,' she flung at him breathlessly.

He said roughly, on ruthless laughter, 'No girl should make such silly statements, Petronella. What man could resist such a challenge?'

'No!' There was terror in her voice as she knew he was going to follow Oliver's example, but with Oliver she hadn't known the old, consuming fear. With Oliver she had known nothing, and from other men she had fled. With Neil she found herself reacting differently again. Perhaps, because he moved so deliberately, it seemed she could only wait numbly for whatever kind of punishment he chose to deal out.

As if aware that she found herself unable to move he took his time. His hands came only slowly to draw her closer as he bent his tall head. He took her lips slowly too, with a punishing sweetness and, as if intent on savouring to the full all she had to offer, forced them apart, exploring the soft contours of her mouth with a sensual technique she knew nothing of. When the first molten waves of sensation began to hit her, a low, anguished moan escaped her, but not even then did he relax his hold. One hand merely threaded through her hair to bring her even closer while his other curved tightly over her pounding breast.

The fire which was sweeping through her veins was swiftly consuming the last remnants of her resistance. It was even stronger than all the fears which had beset her until now. If the fear was still there it was reduced ruthlessly to something negligible by the experienced, superior force of Neil's mouth and arms. There seemed no limit to the feeling which flared through her slight, vulnerable body until every part of her was completely responsive. She knew only a burning desire to be held even closer, to know more, to be able to satisfy him as he was doing her. That it might only end in a singing, blinding release.

The intensity of unconscious longing was such that sensitive tears forced their way at last through her heavily closed lids. Only then did Neil lift his hard mouth from hers, and then it was more like punishment than relief.

He didn't let her go immediately. She heard his sharp intake of breath, but he held her as the ground reeled beneath her, as he traced her bruised lips with one undoubtedly satisfied finger.

'Neil,' she whispered entreatingly, wanting only to turn her mouth into his hand, pleading silently for more of this indescribable kind of lovemaking she could put no name to. She had been half a child until this moment, but Neil had changed all that in fewer minutes than her drugged mind could contemplate. If she hadn't known full awakening it could only be a matter of time. Something smouldering in the back of his eyes promised it.

'Yes, call me Neil. Remember it!' he uttered, his voice coolly devastating. 'You don't have to beg, Petronella, I could go on kissing you until you begged for mercy, and I'm not even sure I would grant it. I have to remember, though, that you could be considered my responsibility. A little salutary lesson, however, could never be held against me. I think you were badly in need of it, my child.'

CHAPTER FIVE

Neil Cameron, like some dark-faced replica of his ancient Scottish ancestor, hustled Petra into his truck with a kind of tersely restrained air about him. Almost, Petra decided, feeling on the brink of mild hysteria, as if she was a child who had been chastised enough for one day but who might still prove fractious. He slammed her door before walking around and lowering himself in beside her. Unexpectedly he turned his head, unfairly, she thought, as he caught her watching him despairingly, her wide grey eyes smudged with the aftermath of too much emotion.

As she waited for some impersonal comment, perhaps about the creek they were just leaving, his next words took her somewhat by surprise.

'We're supposed to be civilised, Petronella. Most times I could swear we are, but it's still a wild country in parts. Don't expect men around here to be gentle lovers. I'd advise you to think carefully, little one, before you plunge out of your depth.'

'I wasn't considering doing anything of the kind.' Tearing her gaze from his, she stared straight ahead, not wanting him to guess she felt as if she were already in, head over heels. If the state of her pulse was anything to go by she might even be irretrievably sunk!

'You'd do well to consider, all the same,' he drawled. 'Oliver Hurd, now, he's a man given rashly to sudden impulses. You might not have got off so lightly if he hadn't been in a hurry. Not if you'd shown him the same degree of response you showed me.'

Pain flicked cruelly as she realised his mocking tones must reflect his opinion of her. Stung, she retorted hotly, 'At least he was gentle, which was acceptable!'

Neil's lips curled derisively. 'With all that Italian blood

77

in your veins how long do you think that would satisfy you?'

Petra's chin went up as she swung around to him again, her heart thudding, not caring to be a target for his savage amusement. 'I thought we were discussing Oliver?'

'You, too, if you're thinking of getting involved in any way.' His eyes slanted from the track to her face, stopping dead on her beautiful mouth before reverting front again. 'You'd be wise to understand he might merely have been laying the bait. I've seen him at work before. He enjoys an amorous flirtation as well as the next man, but he always returns to Janey.'

'Fine!' Petra felt so got at, it made her reckless. Staring at his profile, with its strong, jutting chin, she almost hated him. Defiantly she asked, 'How old is Janey?'

'Twenty-five. You might remember she can give you a year or two.'

'Don't you think she's old enough to take care of herself? Old enough to know it could pay her to be here looking after her own interests?'

'That's just the point, my little beauty. She doesn't often have the opportunity. Her mother has this insatiable desire for travel. She's been around the world so many times she could be dizzy, and she likes Janey with her. It's not Janey you have to worry about, Petronella, but her mother. You see, she wants this match for her daughter with Oliver very much and she'd certainly chop down any foolish little girl who might get in her way.'

Could Mrs Cameron really be as ruthless as her stepson? Petra failed to believe it. Carelessly, because she didn't want Neil to imagine he could frighten her, she shrugged. 'Don't Oliver's feelings have to be considered?'

'Oh, he'll go along with it eventually, if no one interferes. Janey has quite a bit of money of her own which will nicely bolster the Hurds' not inconsiderable coffers. I give her my support as I can quite clearly see that if she was married she would have a reasonable excuse not to be at her mother's beck and call any more.'

'I can't see,' Petra frowned, hesitating as she tried hard

to see clearly, 'why, if Mrs Cameron wants this match, she takes Janey away.'

He swung his head back to her on the straight which ran down to the ranch-house. 'She can't help being selfish, I guess. She keeps insisting Janey is too young to settle down.'

'Do you think she is?'

'I'd say a girl should be settled much younger. There are some who are ready for it,' he said mildly.

Oh ... Petra didn't care for the way his eyes roamed speculatively over her and she shivered as his hand came out to tuck a thick strand of silky hair behind her shell-like ear, as if to see her properly. The slight smoulder at the back of his eyes confused her. 'Well, you needn't think I'm going to throw a monkeywrench in the works,' she cried rashly, trying to keep her eyes from meeting his, from straying to that treacherous mouth, that had made her forget Oliver Hurd even existed!

'Your kind of looks can disrupt anything, Petronella,' he smiled sardonically. 'Of course, I have to remember you're only a visitor.'

A visitor! Petra bit her lip, lapsing into a kind of numb silence and staying that way until Neil drew up in front of the house. Was that a hint she had outstayed her welcome? If he was tired of having David and her around already, how would he react to having them around all the time? For some indefinable reason she wasn't sure if she wanted to be here all the time, now? She had a sudden, irrational craving for a fairy godmother with a magic wand. How nice it might have been to have been able to tell Neil they would be gone tomorrow—to have wished him an extremely polite goodbye!

As things stood, because he appeared to be waiting for some kind of comment, all she could murmur was, 'I'm afraid we've caused some extra work.'

'If you're worrying about that,' he replied, making no attempt to leave her, 'don't. Mrs Allen has plenty help and doesn't mind extra visitors. She tells me you do occasionally make your own bed.'

Petra knew she looked guilty. She must try to remember to do this every day in future. Her wrist had been sore, but it was better now, so she had no excuse. It had been so easy to slip back to the old ways of Redwell, to the days when her father had been able to provide servants to do everything. This wasn't to say she didn't appreciate everything Mrs Allen had done and she hoped Neil didn't think differently. 'I'm not used to being idle, but I never like to be thought interfering,' she said, uncertainly.

'I'm sure you don't,' he agreed smoothly, leaning across her to open her door. The rough feel of his body against hers again sadly depleted her of breath. 'Run along, Petronella,' he commanded, when she didn't move, his mouth twitching as if amused by the too apparent state of her feelings. 'You'd better go see where David has got to, or the two of you will never make it for dinner.'

It was really frightening, Petra thought, a day or two later, how the uncertain state of her nerves seemed to be getting her into situations she might be better out of.

During her discreet searches for the tall cowboy who had rescued her that first day, she had managed to meet quite a few of the other hands. Jake, she discovered, was the real foreman, really Neil's manager. Washed of mud he was an extremely pleasant, well educated man, quite capable of shouldering the responsibilities of the huge ranch when Neil had to be away. It was Jake who had eventually confirmed what Neil had told her about the tall cowboy leaving, so putting an end to her suspicions that Neil had just been making it up!

Unknown to Neil, Jake and she had struck up quite a friendship. It was Jake who had mentioned, when she was wandering rather aimlessly about his office one morning, that one of the younger cowhands was having a sort of coming-of-age party but was disheartened because their one guitarist had gone down with appendicitis.

'Can't Neil supply another,' she had asked idly, 'if one of the other men can't step in?'

'It's not all that important, Petra,' Jake had said. 'No

one else plays and we've such a huge staff Neil couldn't keep up with all their birthdays, although he never objects to them having a bit of a do. When you live as far from town and work as hard as they do, it's not the birthday so much as an excuse to have a party.'

'What's the musician supposed to do?' she had asked carefully.

'Just a few ballads, the odd song. Nothing we can't do without,' Jake had sighed. 'Apart from a few wives, we have no girls here and music helps, somehow, to bridge the gap.'

Petra had looked at him and been startled to hear herself asking impulsively if she would do.

'You?' Jake's bushy eyebrows had risen alarmingly.

'I've had lessons,' Petra had confessed. 'Of course I've never played professionally, but I've heard it said I'm quite good. A whole lot better than nothing, anyway,' she had smiled, while wondering nervously if her old magic was still there. Both her touch and her voice could be sadly lacking in practice. This last year she had only played occasionally, the bleak rooms she had lived in not being very conducive to music in any form. Yet she had still kept her guitar, and when her father had bought it, it had been almost the best that money could buy.

Jake had looked delighted, then doubtful, then, after another moment, relieved. 'Neil will be in town tomorrow evening,' he had exclaimed, as if this explained his various expressions.

'Yes,' Petra had nodded cautiously, and she and Jake looked at each other, both aware of a kind of pact better not put into words.

'He doesn't usually get back until late, sometimes not until the next morning, when he has a night in town.' Jake had supplied the information as if seeking to reassure himself. 'He often dines with a lady friend.'

Wondering why this should hurt so much, Petra had said quickly, 'I'll be here about ten. After David has gone to bed.'

It wouldn't really have mattered about David knowing,

she supposed, as she made her way down to the large shed where the party was held the next evening. But he might have told Cameron and, like Jake, she wasn't sure that he would approve. Neil had left before dinner, his expression rather grim. He had the look of a man determined to seek a little diversion and Petra couldn't altogether blame him. The running of such a big property couldn't allow much time for relaxation, even if such responsibilities appeared to sit lightly on his broad shoulders. He was bound to have plenty of women friends only too ready to supply the sophisticated companionship he sought.

Petra confessed honestly to herself that it wasn't his disapproval she had feared so much as the possibility of a direct order forbidding her to go. In the mood he had been in she didn't doubt he might have put his foot down, even though she was convinced Jake wouldn't have allowed her to take part in anything that wasn't wholly decent. He was older and entirely responsible and hadn't he assured her that most of the wives would be there?

They were—and made Petra very welcome and glad she had been brave enough to come. Their warm, simple gaiety made her realise how starved she had been of young company over the past year and she responded happily. The shed had been swept out and decorated to some extent and was brightly lit. There was a delicious birthday cake and she was given a large slice of this along with some other light refreshments before she was allowed to get out her guitar.

It seemed silly to hope rather anxiously that she might be pleasing, but she hadn't the faintest idea, before she began to sing, just how delighted everyone was going to be. She had dressed in her long skirt and a frilly, low-necked blouse, and she stood, a slight figure in the shadows, her hair, as softly shining as a child's, falling in tumbled curls about her shoulders. She looked like some beautiful young nymph and her voice was altogether charming with a sweet, low-pitched magic, a hint of sensuous huskiness which held her audience spellbound.

Being slightly out of practice, she had a rest after the first half hour before continuing again. She sang some lilting Gaelic ballads, then some middle-of-the-road contemporary songs, and the next hour flew. As she played on she could almost feel the odd tensions of the last week draining from her, or maybe she relaxed knowing that Neil was in town, two or three hours' drive away.

There was unfortunately nothing to warn her that Neil was not. She didn't see him slip into the back of the shed as she was singing so she missed his narrow-eyed surprise which levelled off after a split second to an expressionless, if keen, surveillance. If she had glanced at Jake's face she might have guessed there was something amiss, but he failed to attract her attention and he dared not conspicuously interrupt.

From the contemporary songs, which took on another dimension the way she sang them, she changed to Western ones. She had found some sheets of these arranged for the guitar and to her delight everyone joined in the chorus. She found *The Streets Of Laredo* and *Home On The Range* went down well and finished with *The Night Herding Song*.

There was much shouting for more but, suddenly, she didn't want to go on. Her throat had a slight ache to it and she knew it was time to stop, yet in spite of Jake's protests they wouldn't listen. The cowboys crowded around her as if they had found a valuable new acquisition and had no intention of letting her go. Petra laughed, but she barely knew how to cope with them when they all talked at once.

'I think the girl has had enough, boys,' Neil's voice cut through the chorus of noisy pleading for her to sing again. 'Maybe she'll oblige another time.'

'Neil!' Petra's eyes widened with dismay which, even though she disguised it quickly, must have been obvious to all.

'Yes, Neil!' he ground out, for her ear alone, as he reached her side, laying a proprietorial hand on her arm. His eyes glinted, but he didn't seem particularly angry, unless he, too, was disguising things. 'Put your guitar away, Petronella, and say goodnight.'

But not even the boss was allowed to escape that easily.

Like Petra he was given a drink and pressed to take refreshments. These, she was surprised to find, he accepted, but he didn't let go of her arm. While he downed his drink he kept her by his side and exchanged a few words with Jake. It was only his fingers digging into her soft flesh which gave her any hint of his true feelings. This subtle cruelty, when he was so charming to the young wives who collected to talk to him, kept Petra almost buoyant with hidden indignation.

'I suppose you just stumbled into that crazy bunch?' his voice was pitched low as he nodded towards the men as they left a while later.

'No.' Confession wasn't easy when she felt so light-headed, almost as if she had drunk much more than two glasses of that potent stuff they called harmless liqueur.

'Jake's suggestion?'

'No, he had nothing to do with it. At least,' she confessed truthfully, 'he just happened to say that their regular entertainer was in hospital having his appendix removed.'

'So you felt forced to replace him?'

She hated his sarcasm! She tilted her rounded chin, a small enraged goddess. 'I didn't have to do anything. I'd almost forgotten I had my guitar. It seemed silly not to offer, although I'll admit it wasn't anything I had in mind. It just sort of tumbled out, but surely there was no harm? They seem a very pleasant bunch.'

'Sure they are, Petronella, but even the nicest men can get indiscreet after consuming too much of that stuff they're drinking. Their wives know how to manage them, but you don't. Jake should have known better—so should you. I wonder how you ever survive, having no one to look after you!'

She subsided, having a faint suspicion it suited him to exaggerate a little, yet there was still a niggling fear. 'You won't say anything to Jake? I shouldn't want him to think I'd blamed him for anything.'

He ignored this. 'I'll certainly have a word with him.'

'Please?' Her thick lashes fluttering anxiously, she gazed up at him.

'How sweetly you plead, Petronella. It really pains me that the answer still has to be no.'

Unhappily she subsided. She might as well accept what everyone else did. 'You're the boss, I suppose.' She tried to speak flippantly.

'Never doubt it, lady!'

How could she when he stalked by her side, as adamant as his towering Rockies! 'I thought you'd be staying in town,' she muttered ingenuously.

'Perhaps I suspected something afoot,' he retorted coolly. 'I feel there's a certain telepathy between us, don't you? A kind of sympathetic awareness.'

That wasn't how she would describe it! 'I wasn't even thinking about you,' she said, too quickly.

He jeered, and with his next words her heart almost failed her. 'You think of me most of the time, Petronella, if I've yet to find out exactly why.'

She choked, 'You're imagining things . . .'

'I don't think so, but as you're intent on denying it I must just wait and see. You could be right.'

There was silence as he guided her around a dark corner and with this brief respite from his too discerning tongue her heartbeats slowed. She prayed he might never know why her thoughts centred almost completely on him, but she knew the day couldn't be far off when she must tell him!

'You play very nicely, Petronella,' he complimented her. 'Would you sing for me one evening?'

'I'd rather not.' Just to imagine having his concentrated attention like this made her shake, even noticeably. To refuse might seem ungracious, but she couldn't help it.

He halted at the white railings as they came to the house and she seemed to have no alternative but to pause beside him. The air was still warm after the heat of the day and there was a gentle softness about the night, a caressing quality in the wind on her hot cheeks that made her think poignantly of England.

Suddenly, weirdly to her ears, came the wildly pitched cry of a coyote. 'Ugh!' Nervously she stepped nearer the

tall man by her side. 'They startle more than scare me,' she
exclaimed, as Neil laid a lightly comforting arm around her
shoulders.

'That's sensible.' He made no effort to remove his arm
and a sardonic smile faintly touched his mouth as he
turned towards her, his gaze sliding down the low front
of her blouse, to where a glimmer of starlight showed
momentarily a shadowed hollow. 'You're very attractive,
Petronella, as I believe I've told you before. Maybe you
thought to give the men a treat, but the next time you per-
form for them I should advise you to wear something rather
more decorous.'

'You're beastly!' She felt it and couldn't stop herself
from saying it. It was Neil who made her conscious of her
figure, not his men! Miserably she knew he was right, of
course, about the blouse. Like the rest of her wardrobe she
had purchased it as it had been a bargain. She hadn't
thought the slightly suggestive cut of it would matter. She
hated the way Neil always seemed to manage to spoil everything for her. She could swear he mostly did so deliberately! 'I hadn't much left to choose from,' she cried, her
cheeks pink as she jerked away from him. 'I could scarcely
go in my jeans! Besides, you make it sound worse than it
is. Plenty of girls out for the evening wear much less than
what I've got on.'

'Ah, yes—the depleted state of your wardrobe.' He
didn't appear greatly perturbed by her agitation. 'I'm going
to Toronto tomorrow,' he said unexpectedly. 'If you're
thinking of going home why don't you go there with me?
I could show you around before putting you on a plane.'

'No!' Her eyes must have shown some of the panic she
felt at his suggestion, but she lowered them swiftly. 'I
mean, would you mind if we stayed here a few more days?
David looks so much better.'

'But not you, Petronella.'

'How do you mean ...?'

His eyes, on her face, moved only slowly, as if examining every feature separately. 'Daily you're looking more
haunted. Sometimes I'm convinced you have a lot more on

your mind than you're disclosing. I thought perhaps a change of scene, but if you'd rather stay on the ranch— well, that's up to you.'

He sounded courteous but restrained, as if this wasn't what he personally wanted at all. Petra knew it wasn't really what she wanted herself, now, but it was too late to try to alter much at this late hour. Circumstances were too irrevocably against it. How could she confess she hadn't enough money left for one fare back to England, let alone two? She realised she couldn't stay here indefinitely without some sort of showdown. When Neil returned from his visit to Toronto she must put her plans before him. She also realised, having come to know him, that they might not succeed, but she must try. She couldn't think what she would do if she failed, but surely he wouldn't throw them out on the street? Once David's future was settled satisfactorily she would promise to leave and find a job. After David was safe it wouldn't matter all that much what became of her.

'You don't really want me, do you?' No matter how much it hurt, or how unwise it was to ask, wasn't it better to have confirmation of how he felt?

Indifferently he laughed dryly while his arm, just as casually, it seemed, once again encircled her taut shoulders. 'I enjoy having guests when I can spare the time to entertain them properly,' he drawled, with what Petra might have put down as a hint of evasiveness if she hadn't known he was too direct to indulge in such a vice.

'I'll tell Mrs Allen and Jake to look after you,' he continued lightly, not adding, as she guessed, that he would leave orders she was to sing at no more parties, even if pressed.

'I might be bringing my stepmother back with me. Janey, too, of course. Janey will want to see Oliver.'

In other words, keep off the grass! Petra, while not so adept at reading between the lines as Neil, received the message quite clearly! Mutinously she stared up at him, feeling his attraction even through his ruthlessness. Why did he have to look so like her loved Cameron, the one in the portrait, while the brutal truth was that here was a man who considered her a stranger, one he would dearly like to be rid of!

But even as she stared his bleak face changed and he smiled down at her. 'My beautiful Petronella,' he teased, 'how would my Scottish ancestors have dealt with you? No doubt, from the tales I've read, there would have been at least one among them who would have carried you off to his fortresslike castle and had his way with you. I'm descended from extremely virile men, I believe.'

Petra flinched, the glint of devilry behind his smile forcing her to review her former impression that he knew little or nothing about his forebears. 'People weren't civilised anywhere in those days,' she retorted weakly.

As if he could actually see the high flush on her cheeks and had a fancy to see it deepen, he said suavely, 'What makes you think our feelings have changed so very much? Men still have the same ravaging instincts and women, mostly, still appreciate this.'

'Some women might!'

'When I look at you, Petronella, I feel something very predatory stirring. Don't you think I'd like to take you off to some place where no one could find us?'

Her breath caught in her throat to even think of it and all her stomach muscles seemed to tense painfully—as perhaps he intended. Even her mind, usually fairly nimble, seemed shot through with a sharp, stinging light, not allowing anything but an inane cry, 'I shouldn't let you!'

'Oh, you'd scream to begin with, but not for long, I'm thinking.'

He was merely trying to provoke her. A punishment, perhaps, for entertaining his men without asking his permission. Or maybe, for refusing to go with him to Toronto. She must ignore him. Yet no matter how she tried she couldn't ignore the curious tension which seemed to exist between them. For her part there was a feeling of being strung out on mind-taking electric wires each time Neil concentrated his steely glance on her. The crazy impression remained, even as she attempted nervously to rationalise it, that if he cared to exercise a little pressure she could go completely out of control. Maybe he was right about men and women sharing the same basic impulses, but surely, with a modicum of forethought there was nothing that couldn't be kept in check!

Sensibly she decided to take no notice of his coolly annoying observations. She shook her fair head and smiled lightly at him. 'I think I'll go in now. Will you be gone before I'm up in the morning?' Neither her smile or what she said was altogether to her liking, both tending too much towards the audacious, considering her circumstances, but she didn't know what else to say or do.

'I expect to be, Miss Sinclair,' he was watching her with a kind of taut amusement. 'While I'm gone you might give some thought to your obviously conflicting desires. To hear you talking I'd have thought you'd have jumped at the chance to escape from the ranch and me. Yet here you are, all set, it seems, to stay longer—and I will be back, Petronella, never doubt it!'

'I don't know what you're talking about!' her voice was low and urgent as if she was forcing herself to believe it.

'Oh yes, you do,' he was staring down at her small shocked face, 'or if you really don't, should I make myself clear?'

'Please,' she protested feebly, not ready to admit anything like what he implied. 'I don't think either of us will profit from such a conversation.'

Not conceding her this, he went on, 'Other mysterious aspects of this situation aside, I'm of the opinion that the warm blood of the South—your mother's—invades your so attractively virginal body but that the coolness of a more northern climate rules your head. Have little doubt, Petronella, if there's to be a fight between the two, which one is going to win.'

'Neil Cameron,' she cried, as he stung her with vengeance, 'I'm your cousin!'

He grinned then, his teeth glinting white through the darkness. 'A lot of nonsense.'

'Then you don't believe me?'

'I believe it all right,' his voice was mocking. 'It was perhaps so in the beginning, but too long ago to put any obstacle between you and me.'

She glanced up at his tone and the light caught her wide startled eyes. He reached out suddenly and jerked her against him while the moon danced in wicked glee over his broad shoulder. Then his head, bending over her, blotted it out into a darkness that terrified as his mouth crushed ruthlessly on to hers. He pressed her closer, bending her slowly backwards, ignoring her mute plea for mercy as her slender body was caught against the steel of his arm and the soft skin of her mouth was bruised and broken. Her mouth hurt, but there was also a fire, like some molten lava running through her, making her suddenly cling to him despite the pain. She seemed incapable of any physical resistance as his mouth dealt ruthlessly with her trembling, shaking lips, as if he was practising all the skill at his command. Helplessly she was tossed on the tide of her clamouring senses, the expertise of his lovemaking which seemed to overpower everything else.

When he let her go, somewhat abruptly, she was so bemused she could only stare at him witlessly for the space of hour-long seconds. He appeared to be in no hurry to do anything but look back at her, even if his rather threatening regard was of a somewhat different nature from hers. Petra felt herself growing hot and cold under his light scrutiny which seemed to intimate that everything was going his way, as he had intended all along. His voice when he spoke was low, almost amused, the casual timbre of it raising inside her a near anger that subdued slightly the chaotic state of her feelings.

His hand went smoothly to brush the tumbled hair from her hot forehead, deliberately tantalising. 'If I kissed you again, Petronella, you might even confess to looking forward to my return with no other prompting.'

Petra flinched as though she had been struck with the sword of her own folly. Yet the grey of her eyes darkened to a near violet as she grew afraid, but whether of Neil or herself she wasn't sure. 'I ...' her voice faded weakly.

Words could never come easily when one was so churned up inside. Only one thought got through—she couldn't afford to really quarrel with him. Maybe he had inadvertently shown her the way to get what she wanted, if her nerve held. Who was she to grumble if all she need part with for future security were a few light kisses? She tried not to recall that the kisses she had just exchanged with him had been far from light. With determination she forced herself to go on. 'Naturally I shall look forward to your return, Neil.'

'Naturally,' he echoed dryly, looking far from impressed. 'One day, Petronella, if you stay much longer, I might be tempted to change all that dignified coolness, so be warned!'

David seemed to miss Neil much more than she did. Or this was what Petra tried to convince herself. David, even in three short weeks, seemed to have lost a lot of his pallor. He had put on some weight and was beginning to look quite sturdy again.

'I like it here, Petra,' he told her eagerly, one morning before he went off with Jake. 'I'm not sure if I'd care to be a rancher exactly, but I would like to stay in Canada. Neil says the time to emigrate is when one is young, like you an' me.'

'Did he actually say—me?' Petra heard herself asking, a hesitant catch in her voice.

'Sure he did!' David was already adopting phrases. 'Have you asked him if we can stay? I mean all the time, Petra?'

'Well, no, not yet.' Even to talk about it like this seemed to present an insurmountable obstacle, whereas before she had suggested confidently it was just a matter of time. 'But I'm going to, when he gets back from Toronto,' she said hurriedly, in a little rush which seemed to take a lot of courage, seeing that Neil was hundreds of miles away. Why did she, whichever way she glanced, seem to see his spectral presence looming over her? 'Would you like to go to boarding school here?' she asked, as if unconsciously seeking loopholes. If David was very much against it ...?

'Oh, yes, I would!' David's smile lit up his face but not Petra's spirits. 'Just like Prince Andrew, and we all know how he enjoyed it. It would be super!'

Petra smiled, in spite of herself. 'I'm not sure you could go there, but there must certainly be similar places.'

'But only if you were here during the hols, Petra.' David's sunny expression changed warily. 'If you were going back to England I couldn't stay here on my own.'

'No, darling,' Petra hastened to reassure him, recognising that he still had a long way to go before the damage of the past year could be put right. It wasn't that his schooling in England had been at fault—it had been that too sudden transition from middle-class comfort into near-poverty, on top of the horror of losing his father. 'If you go to school here,' she promised quickly, 'I'll stay too.' It was a wild promise, she had no clear idea how she was going to keep it, but it seemed worth it to see the new contentment on his face. Somehow she would manage it, she whispered to herself. Somehow ...?

She realised she couldn't be blamed when Oliver Hurd turned up, later in the day, and didn't know why she should feel suddenly guilty, as if once again Neil was by her side, silently rebuking her.

'Neil's away,' she exclaimed, jumping in a confused fashion to her feet, leaving the grand piano which she hadn't been able to resist trying out. Neil hadn't forbidden her to use this, perhaps because he hadn't known she played. She had no idea how attractive she looked, her face flushed from her exertions, her fair hair tumbled in a gleaming cascade.

'I know,' Oliver smiled with obvious satisfaction. 'I thought I'd come over and stop you from feeling lonely. Go on playing, Petra,' he pleaded wistfully. 'I happen to be quite fond of good music in spite of my rough exterior,' he joked.

Petra laughed, feeling immediately more comfortable with him than she did with Neil, but she firmly left the piano. Shades of Neil, stalking in unexpectedly and find-

ing her entertaining Oliver, would never allow a natural
performance. Besides, as with her guitar, she considered
she was sadly out of practice, and Oliver was only one
man, not two or three dozen cowboys who stamped and
joined merrily in the chorus, hiding the odd mistake.

'Neil's gone to Toronto.' Oliver might know, but it
could do no harm to mention it herself. 'He'll probably
bring his sister home with him. I believe she's your rather
special friend.'

Oliver helped himself to a drink and sat down before
replying, apparently having no qualms about making himself comfortable in his neighbour's house, even while he
was absent. 'Seeing that we've known each other since we
were rocked in our cradles, I expect it's inevitable that
everyone should think so,' he rejoined dryly, his eyes on
Petra's uncertain face. 'She's apt to be overruled by both
her mother and Neil. I don't think she's ever allowed to
consider how she feels,' he added, even more sardonically.

'Don't you think that girls with that kind of tempera-
ment make the best wives, though?' Petra was somewhat
startled to hear herself asking.

She needn't have worried about indiscretion. Oliver
merely glanced at her moodily. 'For Neil, maybe. He always likes to be top dog, but for myself I'd appreciate a bit
more authority. Don't get me wrong, Petra,' he muttered,
catching her faint air of bewilderment, 'the way I see it
my wife must be able to give me quite a bit of help. I
really do need a girl with your kind of spirit, one who
wouldn't let me forget I have work to do.'

Petra swallowed, not knowing whether to be vexed or
pleased. 'Do I strike you as a kind of martinet?' It wasn't
exactly flattering!

'Of course not!' Oliver was swiftly repentant. 'But you
have plenty of guts. Neil would simply crush a girl like
you, while I would encourage her. Often I long to meet
someone who'd be quite prepared to take some of the
weight off my shoulders. Don't you see?'

Petra thought she did, only too clearly. Oliver Hurd
might be a comparatively wealthy young man, but he was

also a weak one. He wanted a wife who would look after him, not the other way around. Someone very prepared to run after him, to see to his every comfort. 'Perhaps you're mistaken about Janey,' she said tentatively. 'I mean, if both her mother and brother are invincible surely some of it must be in Janey? Perhaps it's too long since you really looked at her?'

CHAPTER SIX

'No,' Oliver grimaced ruefully, having no such illusions, 'she takes after the old man. He was always the weak one of the family, it was common knowledge, in case you think I'd be too young to have known. Neil is entirely different. He was still in his teens when his father died and he's built the place up into what I'd be willing to bet is almost a millionaire's spread out of what must have been an out-size mortgage.'

Nervously Petra shuddered, as she averted her eyes from Oliver's lounging figure. How had she hoped to get the better of a man like that? Herself, a mere girl, whom Neil Cameron could probably snap with two of his steely fingers! 'What about Mrs Cameron?' she stammered.

'Neil's own mother died when he was small and the second Mrs Cameron didn't arrive until some years later. I don't think anyone will ever have known exactly what Neil thinks of her, but he certainly keeps her in luxury. She likes to travel, so I guess this keeps her content. She's rarely at the ranch.'

'But this is her home, surely?'

'Baby!' Oliver laughed lazily. 'You realise you're asking me an awful lot of questions which Neil might, not unreasonably, resent. You could be wiser to put your queries to him, if only to be sure of getting the right answers. Don't tell me you're scared of him?'

'What,' she faltered, colouring faintly, 'makes you think that?'

'I've seen him at work, his manner isn't always encouraging,' Oliver shrugged resignedly. 'Sometimes I wish I were more like him. He goes right after what he wants and says exactly what he thinks. If I had only the half of his proficiency I'd be satisfied.'

That wasn't how Petra would have described it! 'Arrogance, don't you mean?'

'I might at that!' Oliver looked surprised, even appreciative. 'Don't tell me I've met a woman unwilling to sing his praises?'

For some reason Petra didn't want to decipher that. 'He's been very kind to David and me,' she said belatedly.

'I don't imagine he finds it very difficult to be—kind to you, Petra,' Oliver mocked dryly. 'Now, are you going to invite me to stay for dinner or must I go home hungry?'

It wasn't her place, Petra felt, to ask him to stay at all, and she said so. But she also said she would go and see if Mrs Allen could make dinner stretch for three. This was all she could promise to do about it. When Mrs Allen told her she could manage this nicely she felt defeated. After all, in Neil's absence, mustn't Mrs Allen be in charge? Neil had certainly not entrusted this privilege to Petra. Whether or not Mrs Allen approved of Oliver staying, Petra couldn't say. Mrs Allen must surely know all about Neil's hopes for Janey and Oliver, but she passed no other comment than that it would be nice for Petra to have company.

And company Petra did have during the following days. Oliver appeared regularly at the ranch, as if he considered it his duty to entertain Petra while Neil was away. He did entertain her, there was no doubt, as he had, like Neil, been around and could talk very amusingly. Twice he took David and her for a short foray into the foothills and sometimes they all went swimming in the lake, one of the many beautiful stretches of water which dotted the area. On these occasions Petra took picnics which Mrs Allen provided, and when she joined David and Oliver in the water she wore a brief swimsuit which she had fashioned from a short length of material, again supplied by the housekeeper. Altogether Mrs Allen seemed very willing to oblige when Oliver was around. Petra hoped uneasily she was wrong in the sudden impression she got one day that the woman was doing her best to throw them together.

She was convinced she was just being silly, until one evening after dinner when she followed Oliver into the kitchen. He had insisted on seeking their coffee himself and she fancied she overheard Mrs Allen telling him the young English miss liked him a lot.

Oliver's 'I'm sure you're mistaken, Mrs Allen' had been reassuring enough to squash Petra's dismayed indignation and she had crept quietly away so they wouldn't know she'd been there. It was only later that her suspicions had returned. That same evening Oliver, having stayed later than usual, had wanted to kiss her before he left, and she had had to work very hard to convince him she didn't share his amorous inclinations.

'You mustn't forget you're Janey's special friend.' In the struggle to free herself her arm bruised darkly because Oliver was strong and determined. 'Neil wouldn't like it if Janey got hurt.'

'Always Neil!' Oliver sneered with patent resentment, 'A dozen times a day you mention him, Petra. Are you so scared of him?'

'No, of course not!' Petra had denied it breathlessly. 'But I am a guest in his house.'

'Janey and I have no special arrangement,' Oliver had gone on more soberly, 'so whatever Neil thinks, it's not important, not completely, anyway.'

Petra noticed he didn't wholly rule out Neil's opinion, but Oliver, she had discovered, rarely held explicit views of any kind. He was easy going to the point of being easily led, very malleable. She didn't think anything would ever go very deep with him and realised, because of his carefree outlook, she could be worrying herself unnecessarily regarding Janey. Oliver was merely being friendly. She had no reason to be alarmed, not even when he looked at her with something in his eyes she couldn't define. It was possibly just a passing attraction, the novelty of her being from overseas.

She had warded Oliver off with a light smile, but even as he had accepted his dismissal tolerantly he had whis-

pered something about the next time. Cautiously Petra had
resolved there wouldn't be a next time as she had bade him
a sober goodbye.

That had been the night before last. Now he was back
again, pleading with Petra to forgive him and come swimming, and, because it was another day and she was feeling
strangely reckless, she agreed. From the kitchen, with its
huge cupboards and freezers, she collected and packed refreshments and drove out with Oliver to the lake. She
wasn't sure if she would actually swim for at the last
minute David had decided he would rather go with Jake
and Petra found herself uneasily aware that in coming
out here alone with Oliver she might displease Cameron—
if he ever found out! Which, she tried to persuade herself, wasn't likely.

For all her resolution to behave circumspectly the heat
of the afternoon and the warmth of the lake defeated her
eventually. Regretting that her two-piece was so brief, she
whipped off her clothes behind a concealing bush and put
it on. Without glancing more than once to the spot where
Oliver lay drowsily recumbent she plunged into the water.
Grateful that if nothing else she was an excellent swimmer,
she struck out happily for the island which lay about a
hundred yards off shore. The lake in parts was ringed with
cattails and bulrushes, reeds and whitetop grass, and some
dabbling ducks flew off as she approached them. Great
flights of wildfowl, Cameron had told her, moved into this
area in springtime, this being on the edge of the most
famous nesting grounds for ducks in North America.

Through the soaring bluestem grass she watched some
pintail and mallard who didn't seem aware of her presence.
So absorbed was she that it wasn't until she reached the
island and Oliver caught her up that she realised she had
made a mistake in ever coming. During the hour they
had sat on the sandy grass beside the truck he had scarcely
taken any notice of her. He had slept in the heat of the
sun, only talking occasionally, but in coming to the island
she had perhaps seemed to issue an invitation.

'Petra!' he panted, as she dragged herself up on to the pebbly beach away from him. 'Come here!'

'No ...' she turned, telling herself she must speak coolly. Hysterics might only incite him further, if the thickness of his voice was anything to go by. 'Behave yourself, Oliver,' she tried to laugh lightly.

Unfortunately he wasn't to be so easily deterred. His arm went out, catching her around her waist, pulling her excitedly against him, 'Petra,' he breathed, 'you don't know how you affect me, dear. I want to marry you. I've never seen anyone to match you—I don't suppose I ever will!'

Stunned, Petra forgot all about running as she stared up at his eager face. 'Oh, no!' Nothing could have gone this far, so out of hand! She didn't love Oliver—she didn't even like him touching her; hadn't she a bruise to prove it? Numbly she glanced down at her arm, listening to him repeat his wild proposal. What, oh, what would Neil say? And how about Janey? Wasn't this going to spoil everything for everybody if she couldn't talk some sense into Oliver!

Something of what she was feeling must have got through to him as he said fiercely, 'You don't have to be so surprised, dear, you've been pleased enough with me lately. I'll look after you, Petra. I'm not much of a guy, I know, but I have money. I can support you, if this is what you're waiting to hear. I expect this is how it's done in England?'

Almost Petra smiled. 'I don't think we're quite so mercenary. I'm sorry, Oliver,' she gulped, 'I couldn't marry you.'

'Why not?' he asked sulkily.

'It wouldn't work,' she replied, her eyes meeting his pleading ones urgently, as she tried to wriggle discreetly from his grip. Momentarily, as if the impact of her refusal dumbfounded him somewhat, he let her go. If she could reach the water again she might just beat him to the other side? Properly dressed, he might cool down and she wouldn't be so vulnerable. He might be more willing to listen to sense. She might convince him he could feel noth-

ing but a simple infatuation. She was ashamed to realise
that the situation here, with her parading the way she was,
was rapidly going to his head.

'Oh, no, you don't!' About to make a run for it, she
despaired when he caught her, laughing as he guessed what
she had in mind. 'All girls need convincing,' he muttered,
his arms tightening. 'Once I've kissed you, you might want
me to do it again.'

Hard as she struggled it was impossible to evade his
searching lips. His arms, if not as strong as Neil's, were
too determined to allow her to escape. His breath
swamped hers and the ringing in her ears became a shout.
A shout to penetrate fright and despair like a crack of
black thunder! Suddenly she felt Oliver pushing her away
from him, swearing softly under his breath, and there before her horrified eyes, standing cynically on the opposite
bank was Cameron!'

It couldn't be true? Maybe a mirage? Or had the strain
of the last moments caused hallucinations? Such things
happened. 'Who is it?' she whispered, clutching unconsciously at Oliver, as if praying to be reassured it couldn't be
him!

'Neil,' Oliver grunted moodily. 'He would turn up!'

'Neil!' Petra still stared, forgetting in her shock that
Oliver's arms were still about her and that, from where he
stood, Neil might easily imagine they were on the brink of
some torrid affair.

Oliver must have forgotten he held her himself, as when
she moved he made no effort to detain her. 'We'd better
get across and see what he wants,' he said, sounding fed
up but rather nervous. 'Don't forget, though,' he called unexpectedly, as she slipped away, 'I'm always here if you
should ever change your mind.'

'I'm sorry, Oliver,' they were the last words she uttered
until she found herself standing in front of Neil, the
water pouring from her soaked hair, down the bikini, which
was sagging drunkenly from her figure, into the ground.

'So this,' he grated, his eyes like flints, 'is how you've
been passing the time while I've been away!' His icy glance

travelled slowly down her, examining mercilessly every inch of exposed, tantalising skin, and it was worse, much worse than it had been after the party. Then, he had been gently teasing; now he was formidable in his acid disapproval. 'It's interesting to see how Oliver affects you,' he continued scornfully, when she trembled so badly she couldn't reply, 'but I'd advise you to get dressed straight away. I'm not taking you back to the ranch half naked!'

She had beaten Oliver to the shore by perhaps two or three minutes, all it had taken for Neil to slay her with his eyes, scorch her with his savage remarks. Now, as Oliver panted up, he had the air of a man menacingly delivering the final blow. 'Good evening, Oliver,' he said. 'Janey is waiting for you at the house.'

For a second Oliver looked dismayed, as no doubt Neil intended he should. Then he shrugged and grinned, seeming to lose his temporary embarrassment, 'I didn't expect to see you back so soon, Neil. It will be nice to see Janey.'

'You'd better be sure,' Neil spoke laconically. Then to Petra, in harsher tones, 'You can follow us in the other truck—when you get some clothes on!'

Oliver hadn't the demeanour of a man going to meet the only girl in his life. Rather he looked as if he was leaving her as he gazed with anxious fondness at Petra's hotly flushed face. 'I'll wait and bring Petra back myself,' he mumbled stubbornly. 'After all, I brought her.'

'So it seems,' Neil was sarcastic. 'I still think you owe it to Janey to come immediately.'

'You may be right,' Oliver admitted mildly, 'but I won't leave Petra.'

'Get a move on, then!' Neil flung the order at Petra curtly. 'I'll give you exactly two minutes.'

She had never been addressed thus in her life and had a sudden, insane desire to slap his hard, handsome face. 'I can easily drive back myself.' With a great effort she subdued her primitive tendencies and turned to Oliver. 'In fact I would rather.'

'Miss Sinclair!' The threat in Neil's voice shocked further dissension right out of her head. 'Please, God,' she prayed fervently as she stumbled towards the bushes, 'don't let him hate me too much! Please don't let him believe it was exactly as it must have looked, over there on the island.'

In spite of the warmth of the evening she still felt chilled even after she had finished dressing. There was certainly nothing to warm her in the arrogant contempt in Neil's eyes as she almost ran back to them carrying her wet swimsuit in her hand. She had forgotten her towel was still in the truck and she hadn't dared return for it. Now, her badly cut clothes clung to her damp body and she felt terribly uncomfortable. The outer discomfort, however, was nothing to what she felt inside.

Neil was seated already in the driving seat, Oliver beside him. He waved Petra behind him, his hand on Oliver's shoulder as he made to get out when she appeared. 'If you're hungry,' he mocked, 'you can eat some of the refreshments you brought. Did you think to feed an army?' The way he said it seemed to imply that she had a nerve helping herself to so much food that didn't belong to her!

About to reply that she had expected David was coming with them and that Mrs Allen had insisted she took a lot as Oliver was always hungry, Petra decided against it. Why try to vindicate herself when he was so determined to condemn her?

She had thought her silence, though he might construe it as sulkiness, might at least put an end to further discussion, but apparently he wasn't finished.

'I don't object to your having a holiday here, but you shouldn't expect me to supply a man to keep an eye on your young brother while you go off and enjoy yourself.'

'I——' She was flung against the side of the truck as he turned it perilously, with a hard scrub of tyres which stirred the dry brown earth into a miniature storm cloud. 'I,' she began again, ruefully rubbing a sore shoulder, 'thought he was with Jake?'

'Jake's my manager, isn't he?' There was no apology for any bruise she might have sustained. It was almost as if he had enjoyed hurting her.

'Yes—but ...' Oh, what could she say? David had told her Jake had asked him specially to go with him and she hadn't really stopped to query his story. She just remembered seeing him going off with Jake and some of the other men on horseback. Neil was right, of course, she was in the wrong over this, it was no use trying to wriggle out of it. 'I'm sorry,' she faltered unhappily, feeling disconcertingly on the verge of tears. Nothing seemed to be going right. If only Oliver hadn't appeared! Now it would be worse as there would be Janey and Mrs Cameron to contend with. What was she to do?

Surprisingly Oliver came to her rescue. He had been so quiet she had imagined his thoughts to be centred exclusively on Janey. He glanced at Neil. 'Don't be too hard on Petra. I persuaded her to come, David too. He was waiting to accompany us when Jake arrived with this story about wild horses in one of the higher canyons. What boy could resist that? I told Jake to take him. It did give Petra a break, a chance to enjoy herself.'

'So I could see.'

Petra, past caring about Oliver's ill-worded finale and Neil's continuing curtness, still flinched even when she didn't reply. She would get a chance later to say as much as she liked, she fancied, while finding no comfort in the thought. Meeting Neil's dark, enigmatic eyes through the driving mirror was like falling into a bottomless pit, so deep were they with unmistakable promise of a frightening wrath to come.

At the ranch he hustled her quickly inside. Oliver followed. With black-browed arrogance Neil didn't spare her a second glance. Petra had managed to half dry her long hair, to get most of the tangles out. Not yet having had the chance to curl, it hung down below her shoulders, the damp straightness of it giving her a startling, urchin-like appearance which Neil viewed dryly.

'I'll go upstairs,' she whispered, her throat horribly tight as she looked down on her creased jeans, reluctant to meet anyone in such a rumpled state.

'No!' his hand shot out cruelly to restrain her as she

moved towards the stairs, 'you come with me.'

Her eyes, wide and slightly tilted, pleaded with him silently.

'Don't worry,' he said grimly, 'you look about ten years old. Apart from ...' He didn't finish, but his glance slid down consideringly as he guided her stumbling footsteps into the lounge. He held on to her as if it was all part of a conspiracy to make it seem she was with him rather than Oliver, and Petra didn't have the immediate strength to resist.

To look at, Neil's stepmother wasn't nearly so frightening as Petra had expected. Janey, too, was a surprise. She was a small girl, without Petra's slim fineness of limb, but she looked soft and very attractive in a kittenish way. And her eyes, Petra saw, were full of undisguised adoration when they rested eagerly on Oliver. Clearly, for all to see, she was in love with him and would take badly to anything which might upset her plans.

They were barely through the door before she flew into Oliver's arms and began kissing him, soft, adoring little kisses which he didn't seem altogether adverse to even if his eyes met Petra's apologetically over the top of Janey's dark curly head as he hugged her close.

Neil, as if endeavouring tactfully to give them a moment to themselves, drew Petra away to be introduced to his stepmother.

It wouldn't have been exaggerating to say Mrs Cameron seemed taken aback at the sight of Petra's pale beauty, which shone quite obviously, even through her untidiness. Mrs Cameron's eyes, no less ruthless than her stepson's, sharpened instantly, although her tone was deceptively mild. 'Neil has been explaining about you, my dear. Your background intrigues me.'

Petra had the impression it might, but for no particularly charitable reasons! She held out her hand, well aware that Mrs Cameron was withholding her immediate approval. The woman had viewed her arrival with Oliver too astutely for it to be otherwise. Recalling Neil's warning that Mrs

Cameron would never tolerate any threat to her daughter's happiness, Petra shivered inwardly.

Mrs Cameron was smart, not much past middle-age, though, as she obviously spent a great deal on her face and figure, it would be difficult to tell. Janey, by contrast, seemed gentle and yielding, but Petra thought Oliver could have been slightly wrong about her being easily led. Petra felt, when Oliver brought her over to join them, that at the back of Janey's eyes lay more than a hint of determination. Quiet people, she reflected, were often stubborn. The old gardener at Redwell used to say this. He'd said the same applied to plants. It was the nondescript ones which usually flourished as they were usually determined not to be pushed out.

Although Janey's smile was much warmer than her mother's she was clearly bewildered when Oliver gravitated to Petra's side. Petra, aware of a returning grimness to Neil's mouth, was acutely embarrassed by his continued attention, especially when Janey so patently wanted him to herself. She begged to be excused to change for dinner and, as the other two ladies were already dressed, Mrs Cameron graciously granted her request. That Oliver was staying appeared to be taken for granted. Wistfully Petra thought of the evenings when she and David had dined with Neil alone. How, after David had gone to bed, she and Neil had talked. If their conversation hadn't always been without tension at least she had never experienced the awkwardness she felt now with Mrs Cameron's coolly critical eyes upon her. It made her shrink unconsciously nearer to Oliver, whereas otherwise she would have sought to avoid him.

All the time she dressed for dinner her thoughts kept returning to that incident on the island. With other company around Oliver was well enough, but to be alone with him was to realise that all her old aversion regarding men still remained. With Oliver it wasn't exactly as it had been with those few men at work who had tried to molest her but, deep down, she still didn't care to be touched. On the island he had asked her to marry him, which surely proved he was entirely honourable, even if marrying him was something she could never consider. She didn't love him, and naturally he belonged to Janey.

Petra didn't know why she should concentrate so fiercely on Oliver and she didn't try to find out. Better he than that other, more formidable personality, Neil Cameron. She breathed his name painfully, hoping she had mistaken the promise of a showdown she didn't look forward to. There was nothing to explain why, for a flickering second, when she had first seen him this afternoon, she had known such a surge of blinding delight. Nothing to tell her why, when she allowed herself to dwell on it, she had experienced a sudden urgent longing to be in his arms again, even to feel the derisive coolness of his lips. Yet his mouth wasn't always cool and there existed a curious magnetism between them which could make nonsense of her dislike of a man's arms.

David and she went downstairs together just as the long shadows were beginning to creep over the lawns, as the sun slipped quietly behind the craggy, magnificent mountains drawing slowly with it the brilliant, panoramic colours of a fading day. David, chatting happily about the wild horses he had glimpsed, was fortunately unaware of the afternoon's more momentous events and was his usual quietly engaging self.

Janey took to him immediately and even Mrs Cameron's eyes lost some of their frostiness as they watched him approvingly, more approvingly than they surveyed his sister. It was Mrs Cameron's clothes, and Janey's, which made Petra conscious that the two outfits she had worn for dinner continually were long past their best. The cheap material hung limply, attracting several surprised glances from both of them which they made no real attempt to disguise. Janey was nice to her in a distant way, but most of Janey's attention was centred on Oliver, whose side she rarely left.

Neil Cameron sat at the head of the table and Petra found her eyes returning to him again and again. He was so like her dark Highlander of the painting that sometimes she could scarcely bear to look away. In deference, no doubt, to Oliver, who was still in his blue denims, he wore casual dark slacks with a shirt and tie. Even without a jacket he managed to look as he always did, elegant and handsome, enough to turn any woman's head.

Mrs Cameron, Petra knew, would have liked to ask her a great many questions, but Neil mysteriously headed her off, although he did it so discreetly that only Petra seemed to realise what he was doing. Why he was taking the trouble to divert his stepmother's pointed curiosity regarding her circumstances, Petra couldn't guess. Or was he doing any such thing? Perhaps he was merely bored and had no intention of listening to a precise description of the area where Petra lived, or what it was like in Hyde Park when it rained. It was more likely, however, that he didn't want to draw Oliver's attention to her any more than was necessary and was doing his best to relegate her to a mouse-like anonymity.

After David left them they had coffee in the lounge and to Petra's dismay Oliver left Janey's side to come and sit by her. All through coffee she was conscious of his gaze and well aware that this didn't altogether please Janey. Oliver even put his arm along the back of the sofa, where it might have seemed Petra had intentionally sat, and occasionally he dropped it affectionately to her shoulder. If Petra could have excused herself and gone to bed she would willingly have done so, but at nine o'clock she could think of no valid reason to escape upstairs.

Eventually, not surprisingly, Janey grew restive as her eyes clouded increasingly with suspicion. She got to her feet, wandering restlessly to the window, frowning as she turned quickly to survey the two on the couch.

It was then that Neil, as if sensing a mild crisis, exclaimed lightly, 'You might have forgotten, Oliver, but there's still your truck to collect from the lake. I forgot to mention it to the men and it would be simpler now to fetch it ourselves.'

'Oh, God, yes ...' with a yawn Oliver stretched ruefully. 'A good job you remembered, Neil. I guess I'll need it later.'

'I think we'll go with you, Petra and I.' Janey's face lit up. 'Petra can talk to Neil while you and I hold hands in the back,' she giggled.

Petra was so startled when the lake was mentioned she could scarcely hide her acute aversion. She didn't want to go there again—well, not immediately. She felt too raw about what had happened on the island, and Neil's wrath. 'I'll stay with your mother, Janey,' she stammered, 'or maybe go to bed. It's almost ten and I'm feeling tired.'

She thought she caught a hint of warmer approval in Mrs Cameron's eyes than had been there all evening. Then Neil spoke again.

'We can't allow that you're tired at your age, Petra. You don't even have to make the effort of fetching a wrap. The night's still warm, so no excuses. If you think I'm risking having no one to talk to while these two have ears for themselves alone, then you can think again!'

Petra lowered her lashes so he wouldn't see her despair. Why did he have to spoil things? 'It's only a few miles,' she protested.

'All the more reason why you should come.' Neil actually smiled as he marched her outside, after pulling her ruthlessly from her comfortable seat. 'Do you have to play so dumb!' he bit out in terse undertones, as Janey and Oliver followed more leisurely.

'Even if I hadn't been here they could still have sat in the back!' she retorted fiercely, under her breath, as he reversed swiftly away from the door.

'I couldn't think of anything more awkward,' he drawled, his voice still low, 'and I've no intention of getting myself embarrassed.'

That would be the day! she thought waspishly. 'I didn't want to go back to the lake tonight,' she protested faintly, making sure that Janey, conversing gaily behind them, didn't hear.

'Sometimes,' Neil drawled cynically, 'it's better to go

straight back—to the scene of the crime, so to speak. To look a bout of foolishness, or whatever, straight in the face almost immediately can often save one from making the same mistake twice. It just has to be driven into your head, sweet Petronella, that Oliver is not for you!'

Petra's fingers clenched tightly into fists and she didn't see his eyes glance narrowly down on them before returning to her pale face. 'What will it take, I wonder, to knock all this romantic nonsense from your head? Oliver seems to have made quite an impression in one short week.'

Ignoring this with a great effort, Petra fell silent, feverishly glad when, as if wearying of whispered undertones, Neil didn't press for an answer. How could she explain that she suddenly felt she couldn't bear to discuss another man while sitting so close to him here? She was too conscious of his every move as he drove the heavy truck ruthlessly through the moon-splintered darkness, of his every breath as he began to whistle snatches of popular tunes in a low key. When he put his arm around her shoulders and drew her deliberately closer she was too bewildered to move away. Did this mean he was sorry for losing his temper earlier, that he wanted to make amends? Feeling it might be easier to go along with this line of thought, she snuggled closer. It was surely wiser than fighting him and when he was being friendly he was quite nice. Sleepily, she realised that this last gesture might merely have been to impress Oliver!

Once at the lake she had thought they would be going straight back to the ranch, but apparently this was not to be so. When Janey suggested they all stroll around it in the moonlight, Neil nodded lightly and said he didn't mind. Petra, her cheeks still flaming with humiliation on being aware that once again she had fallen into one of his little traps, wanted to decline, but was allowed no option.

'A breath of fresh air will help you sleep, Petronella,' Neil quipped, 'even if you don't look over-pale. While these two walk along the shore and catch up on all their news, I'll show you a view of the ranch you won't ever forget. As you're a visitor to our shores we perhaps owe it to you. If you hitch up that long skirt over one arm it shouldn't come to any harm.'

By this time, perhaps because of the many disturbing elements of the day, Petra just didn't seem to have the strength left to argue. A view from any hilltop was inviting, but some dark, cautionary instinct warned her this might not be all that it seemed. No matter—it surely could do no harm to play along. If Neil was so determined that Janey should get what she wanted, hadn't she better help him? By doing this she might even be inadvertently helping herself, and if it only meant climbing to the top of one hill then it shouldn't prove too difficult.

Oliver was the only one to protest mildly and this seemed to merely set the seal on Neil's determination. 'See you,' he grinned sardonically, taking Petra's arm and moving away. He was so arrogantly careless about it that further objections seemed pointless, if anyone had dared proffer them. Soon, as the darkness of the trees engulfed them, Petra heard nothing at all.

She grasped her long skirt, as Neil had instructed, and let him help her over several heaps of large boulders and logs. 'Now,' he smiled, as they traversed the last of them, 'it should be easier. These logs are swept up from the water during storms and the boulders come tumbling down from above to join them.'

'In winter?' she asked, already breathing deeply as the incline grew steeper. How did he imagine she would ever manage this, dressed as she was?

'Sure,' he drawled. 'Winter, in these parts, can be quite something, Petronella. We usually have snow lying for months and the cold is no respecter of persons. Pity the man who has no wife to keep him warm at night, girl.'

The heat was in her cheeks again although she realised he was just taunting her. 'To a man like you that should be no problem,' she retaliated dryly, the wind blowing her hair across her mouth so she sounded as if she might be choking.

His mouth curved at the corner. 'The roads are always

blocked for weeks. It can be very cosy, or it could be with the right company.'

She trembled a little, hopelessly unsure, forced to continue impersonally when the odd inflection in his voice seemed to put everything on quite a different level. 'How do you manage to get out, away from the ranch, I mean?'

'The helicopter, occasionally.'

'So you aren't entirely cut off.'

'No,' she thought he sounded distantly amused, 'but we're often so busy we might as well be. You sound interested, Petronella?'

His jeering taunt flicked her cheek. He couldn't suspect what she had in mind, surely? Her pulse jerked and her fingers curled into her hands in an effort to restrain it. 'Naturally I'm interested,' she rejoined stiffly.

She caught the glint of his mocking smile which seemed reply enough and with the light glint of sky on the hilltop above them, she tried to hurry, to put even the distance of a few yards between herself and this man who could so bewilder her. The first steepness levelled out and thankfully she found she could manage nicely but, try as she might, she still remained only a step in front of him and her pulse, instead of slowing, beat faster.

Not knowing why, she heard herself asking, 'Why couldn't we have gone with the others? Wouldn't it have seemed more friendly?'

Neil's voice came harshly, 'Still hankering after the unobtainable?'

'In what way?'

'Oliver.'

'For heaven's sake!' she burst out, then sobered immediately. 'He could believe he was in love with me, though.'

His snort of disbelief was scarcely flattering. 'You really think that's on—in little over a week!'

Coming from him that was mysteriously painful. 'People have been known to fall in love in less. Even at first sight.'

'Leaving out unpredictable desire, what makes you think you're qualified to make such comments?' he grated.

Disliking his tone intensely, Petra toiled on, thinking how she had been in love with a portrait and then completely disillusioned with the flesh and blood reality. 'No,' she conceded unhappily, 'it's just some sort of attraction.'

'Well, Petronella,' he scoffed softly, 'there has to be something to make the world go around. We have to consider the future generation ...'

Now he was making everything horrid again! Striking into her a kind of fear, a chill, like the sharp call of the lone coyote further down the creek. Janey would hear it and it would be an excuse to cling to Oliver, but Petra knew she would find no such comfort in Neil's arms. It could never be comfort a man like Neil Cameron would be after—would think of supplying, in spite of all his talk of cosy winter nights!

Shivering, all her old nervousness of men returning, she hurried her stumbling feet, not daring to continue such unsettling thoughts. She reached the summit a little way ahead of him but knew this was because he took his time. As she stood in the light breeze it blew her wide skirt against her long slender legs, causing her thin blouse to cling to every soft curve of her figure. It lifted her long silky hair sensuously, but the view was so mind-taking she didn't even stop to consider. Through a gap in the trees she could see away down below in the distance the white, spaced buildings of the homestead. Then spreading wide before it, out beyond the foothills, shadowed and silvered in the moonlight like some limitless waste, the prairies rolled onwards, it seemed, to eternity. Standing here, Petra felt she could be as remote as the moon.

The wind sighed through the tops of the huge pines and there was silence, a wild, scented soul-stirring silence, a reflection somehow of the high Rockies above her, making her feel suddenly very small.

CHAPTER SEVEN

'WELL, what do you think of it?' As Neil came up beside her he put an arm around her as she swayed against the wind, drawing her protectively to him.

Petra stiffened, feeling a tremor go right through her already breathless body. Maybe he was just trying to make up for his former unfriendliness, but when he held her close like this she had no means of coming to terms with the way he could make her feel and she was in no position to oppose him. Her mistake must lie in coming up here with him in the first place, but he had a way of sweeping one along. With her mind she could attain a certain aloofness, but near to him, her body seemed forever to be curving towards him, as if some invisible current drew her to him whether she wanted it or not.

Honestly she tried to answer his question, putting this other aspect from her. 'It's beautiful. No—out of this world. I mean ...' helplessly she tried again, seeking for the right words to describe the riveting panorama before her, 'it's rather like Scotland on a much bigger scale. I can't seem to find the right words and I don't want to sound superficial.'

His breath came warm against her ear as he turned his head. 'I know exactly what you mean. Parts of this country have even the best writers beat. I guess there aren't words, not in our vocabulary, to do it justice.'

To lighten the atmosphere, which somehow appeared to be pressing down on her, she replied flippantly, 'So you wouldn't say I wasn't trying?'

'Not in that direction anyhow.' He sounded sardonic, but his arm tightened. 'I still haven't got you exactly weighed up, but just for the moment I'm not even trying.'

Far from reassuring, this only spelt danger to Petra, who was increasingly aware that in a tight corner she would

have no idea how to handle him. He might hold his suspicions lightly, yet he never let her forget he had them.
And soon he must know!

Nervousness accelerating wildly, she tried to move away,
'I think we should go down now. Oliver——' she had
been going to say 'and Janey' when Neil swung her around
hard, choking the words in her throat before she could
utter them.

'You never give up, do you?' he cut in coldly. 'It leaves
me with no alternative other than to chase all thought of
Oliver from your charming head.'

'No!' she cried, her voice too frail a barrier to protect
her in any way as he put both arms around her and drew
her closer.

'You'd only be wasting your breath if you shouted up
here, Petronella,' he mocked, running his hand through
her moon-gilded hair, tugging gently until her head came
back against his shoulder and he could see her face. Then
his fingers were tracing the line of her cheek, lifting her
quivering chin, holding her in a vice as his mouth slowly
descended.

Holding her so tightly, he must have known her resist-
ence could never be physical, that he hurt her, he waited
until the hard flame of his mouth seared right through her,
and she collapsed weakly against him. It was only then
that his grip eased and one hand slid from her back to
curve the vulnerable softness of her breast. As he heard
her swiftly indrawn breath the pressure of his mouth increased, sensuously.

There was a singing noise somewhere in Petra's ears,
as if from the flame which seemed to be kindling to a blaz-
ing fire within her. She had no means of escaping and now
she wasn't sure she even wanted to. Her heart was beating
so swiftly it was like a pain beneath his probing hand and
the heat under her skin seemed to be increasing alarmingly. But if there was danger she was scarcely aware of it.
She should have been fighting him yet, this close, she had
no defence. Rather, as the ache of longing inside her increased, she only wanted to be nearer. Her arms went up

around his shoulders to curve the back of his head, her fingers aching with a kind of urgent pressure to match his own. Never could she understand why she should be clinging to Neil Cameron like this, but suddenly she didn't care.

He lifted his mouth from hers to explore her slender white throat, to linger and soften on the pulse which beat so frantically at its gently hollowed base. 'What price Oliver now?' he whispered, returning to her face.

Feverishly, it seemed, she no longer wanted to waste time thinking about Oliver. As if instinctively knowing she might never, after tomorrow, be in his arms again, she only wanted Neil to go on kissing her. It was an intolerable sweetness she never wanted to stop and, shamelessly, she invited his wandering lips. 'You don't let me think about him,' she murmured witlessly as he seemed to be waiting for an answer.

His mouth played with hers again, with consummate skill, as if he understood her bewildering degree of response better than she did herself. 'Would you perhaps prefer not to think of him, Petronella? You don't strike me as being half in love with another man.'

And all this was just his way of finding out. The thought filtered through and she should have been furious, but no anger came. She might have been beyond it. The smooth planes of his face were hard, promising nothing, but she could only see so much. She found him suddenly infinitely exciting and she felt her heart leap. 'Just hold me,' she pleaded, wanting much more, but not knowing how to ask.

His hand swept down to the curve of her thigh, as if he gave way, momentarily at least, to the throb of temptation. 'We've come a long way, you and I, in the last few minutes,' he said suavely, and she knew he wasn't talking about their trip up the hillside. 'Are you pleading with me to go further?'

The wind at her back blew her thick lustrous hair back from her nape, exposing the pure line of her head, the coolness of it restoring a little sanity. If the wind wasn't re-

sponsible it must have been what he had just said. Had
she really put herself in such an ignominious position?
'Neil,' there was a broken little catch in her voice, 'you'd
better let me go.'

'I'm damned if I will,' he rasped. 'I like the feel of you
in my arms, and don't try to persuade me you're entirely
indifferent!'

'No ...' She was thankful she could be truthful for
once even if such a confession might spell danger. 'But
that isn't to say ...'

'Stop talking.' Relentlessly his lips closed over hers
again, careless of the hot, dark tide that immediately
flooded over them, sealing them together as he crushed her
tightly to him. Petra felt the pain of knowing every hard
muscle in his body, but this time she didn't attempt to
evade him. He wound her hair like a silk rope, dragging
her ever closer, cruelly bruising with his deep penetration
the soft, quivering contour of her mouth. She was trembling like the aspens they stood under when at last he released her and could only stare at him in a kind of childish daze that had nothing really childlike about it.

As his arms fell away his rejection was so abrupt it
seemed to hurt more than his ruthlessness. The unconsciously tragic query in Petra's wide eyes seemed to drag out
an explanation against his will. 'It would be nice to,' he
said tersely, so that she could never mistake his exact meaning, 'but it could lead to untold complications. You go to a
man's head like strong wine, Petronella. Maybe it's the
Italian in you, but where you're concerned I wouldn't know
when to stop. It might amuse you that I've only just discovered.'

Stunned shock running uncontrollably right through
her, Petra turned blindly away. Was he right? Never before had she been forced to realise the depth of her own
passionate nature. But then this was the first time any man
had kissed her, held her like this. Others had tried, but she
hadn't allowed them to get really near her. Neil Cameron
was the first but he would never believe her. Although,
with his conceit, it might amuse him if she was to confess

that for a few minutes, there in his arms, she might have given him willingly that which she had always held sacred. Without betraying herself with another despairing glance she took herself away from him, to stumble down the mountain.

The next morning nothing seemed any clearer and she could only view Oliver's next arrival, later in the day, with increasing depression. Oliver, it seemed during the next few days, was contriving to become a constant visitor and nobody seemed inclined to discourage him. Mrs Cameron said it was only natural that he should want to be with Janey when she had been away for so long.

Janey, to begin with, seemed very satisfied with Oliver's increasing appearances, and when Petra pointed out quietly that most men had work to do she got very indignant.

'His father doesn't mind him seeing me in the least!' she retorted coolly. 'He likes to run things his way and it suits him to have a son who'll let him.'

'Don't you think sons of Oliver's age should be given some authority? A chance to assert themselves. It can't be good for him, surely, to be allowed so much leisure?'

While Petra hadn't meant to sound so critical she was startled to hear Janey reply softly, 'When we're married that will all change. He needs someone like me to guide him.'

'I'm not sure you're right,' Petra said sharply, without thinking. 'Now if it was me ...'

'But it's not you, is it?' Janey's face had flamed with sudden temper. 'He loves me, not a little interloper like you. You'd do well to remember!'

She flounced away before Petra could reassure her, and feeling not a little sickened by Janey's hurtfully unjust warning, she didn't bother to go after her. Consequently Janey's coolness almost matched that of Neil, and, not unnaturally, Petra found herself turning more and more to Oliver although, certainly, with no romantic notions in her head, even though she did sometimes remind herself that he had, in a mistaken moment, asked her to marry him.

As she had suspected, Janey wasn't nearly so quiet as she seemed, and she seemed to regard Oliver's increasing absorption with Petra with mounting suspicion. It took Petra some time to realise he had taken to watching her exclusively, even when the others were around and, impatient of her own carelessness, she took to avoiding him as much as possible.

Between him and Neil she often felt she was walking a tight-rope above disaster, with Mrs Cameron waiting with cat-like malice below, gleefully anticipating her fall. The showdown with Neil, Petra knew, couldn't be put off much longer, but if she had hoped it could be somehow postponed until Janey and her mother had once again departed it wasn't to be like that at all.

Since the evening on the hilltop Neil had been distinctly unfriendly, so much so that Petra sometimes wondered if he could be the same man who had kissed her so urgently. She was aware that Janey went to him with tales, but these must merely confirm his already voiced opinions. Janey was adamant that Petra led poor Oliver on and, judging from the dour mood Neil was in, he was only too ready to believe it. One thing he made abundantly clear, his sympathy did not lie with Petra. He regarded her with increasing coldness which Petra often felt she could scarcely bear, even if she didn't quite know why.

It should not have surprised her, but it did, that this tense state of affairs should come to an abrupt halt one evening after dinner. Mrs Cameron had retired to bed, almost following David upstairs, pleading a headache. Mrs Allen fussed upstairs after her with tea and aspirin, leaving the four younger people sitting in the lounge alone. Oliver, after Mrs Cameron had departed, begged Petra to play for them and reluctantly, aware of Neil's raised eyebrows, she obliged. She hadn't minded playing for Oliver before, but having Neil watch her broodingly was quite a different matter. It wasn't as if she was particularly good. Her father used to say she was too lightweight and her technique too limited, but then she had never made any pretensions to being professional. She played a little Mendelssohn and Beethoven, which latter Oliver professed to liking, but she felt happy with none of it and as soon as possible gave up. Perhaps it was Janey's silent antagonism that put her off. Twice she had had to delicately cover a rather clumsy mistake and, if the others didn't notice, Cameron's dryly expressive face left her in no doubt that he did!

Crushed, she drooped her fair head, her glossy hair spilling over her cheeks in silky confusion. She felt vulnerable, completely spent, in no way able to search for the answer to Neil's almost open derision. It seemed more than likely that some of her own silent despair had come through in the music, a hint of her silent misery and self-disgust regarding the quite insoluble fix she had got herself into. Neil couldn't know how when she occasionally thought she had succeeded in forgetting for a while it was still there, almost eating her up, like some horrible blight, consuming her mind. She could laugh to recall the mental picture she had had of herself pouring out all her trouble into the ears of a kindly, upright, elderly relation. But now, because of these mistakes she had made all along, there was nothing for it but to bluster her way through to the bitter end. That the end would be bitter she was becoming daily more convinced.

It didn't seem possible that with a list of such mistakes to warn her, she should make yet another. Half distracted by the prevailing coldness in his eyes, she turned from him to smile in an over-brilliant fashion at Oliver. Janey, seeing the instant, reciprocal warmth in Oliver's face, looked ready to burst into tears. Her hands clenched and a small choked sound escaped her as she swung away from them.

In a flash, so that Petra was scarcely aware he had moved, Neil was on his feet and at the piano, his hand curving Petra's slender wrist firmly. 'If the recital's over,' he said smoothly, 'Petronella and I will say goodnight. We have things to discuss and I won't have time in the morning. You must excuse us.' He smiled, but it was a mere twist of his well shaped lips as he jerked Petra none too gently to her reluctant feet and whipped her silently through the door.

'Quite a string of minor accomplishments you have, don't you?' he quipped sarcastically, as he guided her relentlessly down the passage outside, 'and all of them useless.'

Stung by his curtness, Petra stumbled. 'I can cook and ride a horse,' she heard herself protesting incredibly, and she realised none of this might impress him. 'Where are we going?' she asked quickly, trying to cover a hot surge of mortification.

'Some place where we won't be interrupted—or heard,' he added, ominously, 'should you choose to make a fuss.'

Convulsively Petra swallowed, a cowardly fear nearly getting the better of her. He sounded so determined! 'Wouldn't tomorrow do?' she whimpered miserably. 'You've had a long day.'

'Tomorrow never comes, Petronella,' he replied suavely, 'and don't begin searching in that charming head of yours for a contradictory cliché as my patience is rapidly running out!'

Which didn't bode well for any kind of discussion, Petra thought bleakly.

It transpired he was taking her to the office which was right at the back of the house. Petra had only been here once. There was a whole lot of the house she wasn't at all familiar with as Neil had never exactly encouraged her to explore, and not even when he had been away had she done so. Nervous that she might be accused of trespassing she had decided to wait until he asked her to stay permanently. There would be time enough then. Unfortunately, with the arrival of Janey and her mother, everything seemed to have changed. It didn't seem likely now that Neil Cameron would be inviting her to do anything!

Behind her he was closing the office door; it was rather like the knell of doom. There was still a kind of suppressed anger about him that the walk along the corridor hadn't abated. They were alone and this large room was miles away from the main quarters, for the precise reason that

Neil often worked here in the evenings and valued the peace and privacy. Petra found no such reassurance. She felt herself shaking as she watched him turn and stroll over to his desk as if deciding the best way to annihilate her.

Trying too obviously to postpone the evil moment, she queried desperately, 'Did my playing annoy you?'

'No.' His lip curled, as if he realised quite clearly she was playing for time. 'You haven't the scope of a more experienced performer, but then I don't suppose you ever considered making a living from it. It was, like all your other performances, quite eye-catching. I imagine the slight faux pas was merely a reflection of your present state of mind?'

'State of mind?'

'Don't prevaricate, Petronella.' His dark blue eyes glittered dangerously. 'Isn't it about time we had a frank talk? You come here for a couple of nights and stay weeks. I suggested you go with me to Toronto and you refused. I don't want to seem inhospitable, but it isn't convenient for you to stay longer.'

'Because you think I'm after Oliver, I suppose?' Petra's nerve seemed to desert her. She hadn't been going to mention Oliver at all!

If she had unconsciously sought to divert him, she succeeded, but only briefly. He merely observed coolly, 'It doesn't seem worth subjecting Oliver to what looks like becoming a mild infatuation. I also have my sister's interests to consider.'

Foolishly she couldn't leave it alone. 'If I promised to have nothing more to do with him?'

He turned on her then, cruelly grasping her slender arm and pushing up the concealing sleeve to reveal dark bruising. 'Don't tell me that got there by itself.'

Pink flooded her pale cheeks guiltily. 'It—it was an accident.'

'Possibly,' he rejoined silkily. 'I'm sure Oliver wouldn't do it intentionally. But tell me, is this the action of a man without urgent intentions?'

Stubbornly she shook her head, her mind in such chaos

she couldn't think straight, but she did realise that to have Neil in an antagonistic mood would never get her what she wanted. 'I'm sorry,' she whispered, trying to look straight at him, 'but I think you do overestimate Oliver's feelings.'

Whether this completely satisfied him or not, she couldn't say. He remained beside her, even after releasing her arm, nearer to her than he had been in days, and her heart was over-reacting. She could feel it thudding swiftly and rebelled dully that she had a great longing to be in his arms again. Arms which clearly didn't want her.

What he said next confirmed it. 'Supposing,' he drawled dryly, ignoring her last remark, 'we get back to the original point—the date of your departure. I think we'll be able to work better from there.'

This last enigmatic sentence was lost on Petra. Her head was spinning with a kind of blinding shock even before he reached it. She could only flounder illogically when she had meant to sound very cool and detached. 'I'm afraid David and I would like to stay longer.'

He frowned sharply. 'How long?'

Petra's face whitened visibly as she stifled a growing regret that she hadn't the money to promise they'd be gone in the morning. She couldn't bring herself, yet, to place all her cards on the table. In a few minutes, if she remained calm, Neil might—he just might ask her to forget everything and stay, thus saving her the utter humiliation of having to beg. Because she had no illusions now that this was what it would be. 'Surely,' she tried to speak lightly, 'you don't doubt who I am?'

'Petronella,' he exclaimed, on the fringe of a weary impatience, 'I don't altogether doubt who you are. I hardly think you just stuck a pin in a map and landed on me. But how about starting at the beginning? You've built something, I think, from some very basic facts, and I want to know exactly what it is.'

So this was the end. How could she possibly put into words all the maybe unreasonable terrors which had almost driven her here? Once, at the height of her foolish confi-

dence, it had seemed so easy. Would he ever understand?
Helplessly she stared down on the wide expanse of office
floor, finding little inspiration in the rather threadbare carpet.

'Lost your tongue?'

It was amazing how such a sarcastic taunt revived her
flagging courage. Maybe Neil would call it her impertin-
ence, but his derisive tone did give her the strength to go
on. 'David and I can't go home,' she stated baldly. 'We
have no money and no place to go. So I'm afraid you're
stuck with us.'

Her young voice, incredibly clear and pure, sounded
defiant and for a moment he looked furiously beyond
words, utterly astounded. His hands lifted, as if he meant
to shake the life out of her, but when she flinched visibly
they fell again to his sides, in a kind of helpless anger.
Turning from her suddenly, he pointed to a nearby chair.
'Sit there,' he commanded grimly, 'and you'd better be
prepared to confess the lot. I want no more half-truths.'

When Petra, after two false starts, began to talk she
knew she was putting things badly. Everything just
tumbled out, in a most confusing way, guaranteed to impress no one, not even herself. All her carefully rehearsed
speeches seemed to have fled. To start at the beginning, as
he suggested, not being as easy as one might have thought.

'My father went bankrupt,' she stated unevenly, her
eyes on Neil, blank and dazed with the curious shock of
having to put it into words again. 'There was a fire and he
died. Afterwards it was discovered what state his business
was in. His London office wasn't destroyed, of course, and
he'd kept his diaries there. He must have been researching
for years, so his solicitor said. All the details are there of
our family tree. When I was given his personal papers
these were among them, you see, and I thought it would
be a good idea to come over here and live with you.'

'Just like that!' Neil spoke so softly she could scarcely
hear it, but as she caught it faintly, her cheeks flamed.
'How long since your father died?' he asked curtly, as if
they were discussing a shower of rain.

'Just a little time ago.' She fancied she had once told him exactly and prayed, if she had, that he had forgotten.

'Didn't it occur to you that any normal person would have set about earning a living in an orthodox way?'

She couldn't tell him what a failure she'd made of that! Better to let him think what he would. 'It was difficult because of David,' she faltered, finding in his hard demeanour not one hint of softening.

'I might have guessed,' he exclaimed, his mouth tight. 'Maybe I've been even more remiss than you. No clothes to speak of, nothing but two pieces of shabby luggage you obviously picked up in a junk shop. And I fell for it! Don't you know, Petronella,' he leant over her, breathing fire, 'you've managed to make a nice fool of me, something I've never allowed to happen before. My friends might enjoy hearing about it!'

Feeling faint from the force of his dry anger, Petra stared up at him weakly. 'I don't see how anyone could jump to those conclusions.'

'Don't you?' his voice rasped. 'Well, it's nothing I care to dwell on. Just get on with the rest of your story.'

'You just don't understand!' Desperately Petra jumped to her feet, as if standing she might have more impact. 'I— you have so much while David has so little! You didn't have to see him going without, day after day, until I thought he was about to fade away. You don't know what it's been like. And those ...' she had been about to say 'those men', but her voice faltered at the last minute. Never could she bring herself to mention them, not to Neil Cameron. 'If I'd known what you were really like,' she mumbled unwisely, 'I would never have come.'

His mouth stretched in a travesty of a smile, with no mirth in it, and his eyes resting on her distressed white face were grim and cold. 'That's very easily remedied,' he grated. 'I'll pay your return fare to London. It will be cheap at twice the price. Then we can forget we've ever known each other.'

'No!' Her vision blurred, as she stared at him. So it had to come, the time to play her trump card, which wasn't that at all, really. It was more a pathetic, improbable gesture, unlikely to cut any ice with a man like this. 'You can't send us back. David wouldn't survive! Besides, you owe it to us to let us stay.'

'Owe—you?' He was cool, almost insulting, in his sneering disbelief.

'It's true!' Madly she rushed on as caution deserted her, 'Your ancestor borrowed five hundred pounds from mine, who was his brother, and never repaid it. All those years ago—with interest it must surely amount to an enormous sum now. Or at least,' she challenged breathlessly, 'enough to keep David and me here for a year or two and to send him to a good school.'

'Why, you mercenary little——!' He called her something to make her ears burn. Without regret, or so it seemed, he was beside her in two strides, this time his hands showing no reluctance to grasp her shaking shoulders. 'What proof have you? And what sort of mind, to plan this all out?'

She could feel his fingers digging into her tender skin with the force of his wrath and it took every bit of willpower she had to defy him. 'It's all there, in black and white, indisputable records, handed down through generations. It was never repaid.'

'And you intend that I should do this? In spite of your grand theories this sort of thing is nearly always impossible to prove. It's ridiculous to even discuss it!'

'Oh, I know it's highly improbable that any court would uphold it legally, but that shouldn't stop you from trying to be a man of honour. I thought you would have wanted to compensate for your ancestor's obvious oversight.'

With his face so black he resembled the Cameron in the painting closely and Petra felt more than a twinge of fright run right through her. For a moment she felt she was back in those wild Highland days with the skirl of the pipes, wild music in the background of dark mountains, and a furious Highlander about to strike her.

If Neil had such primitive inclinations, he managed to control them partly, only releasing his anger through his voice. 'You can't be serious! You imagine I'd let myself be blackmailed—for this is what it would amount to, for a few paltry pounds? Threatened into keeping you in idle luxury for the rest of your life, with no strings attached. You must be crazy!'

'Your friends mightn't think so if news of this got out.' Petra strove to speak coolly. That her voice shook appeared to go unnoticed. She quivered even more to see his temper increase. It was of the cold variety, infinitely more frightening, she had always found, than a raging torrent. His icy gaze sliced into her, almost cutting her in two as she made a desperate attempt to stand up to him, to sway him in any way possible—even if, for David's sake, it meant swallowing every last scrap of pride.

Neil jeered at her with a marked lack of apprehension for her last wild threat, 'If you want to broadcast this, you little tramp, just go right ahead. You'll be the laughing-stock, if anyone is—if anyone even bothers to stop and listen. That first time I set eyes on you, when you were standing beside your wrecked car, I knew you spelt trouble! It's the first and last time I'll not pay some attention to my intuition.'

Petra stared at him aghast, scarcely aware now of his hands abruptly leaving her shoulders. 'You saw me by my car? You mean you were—are——?' she couldn't continue, she was so shocked.

'You're too astute,' he mocked, never intending to spare her. 'I was the tall cowboy you talked down to. You were such a starchy little madam I decided to see how far you would go. I certainly never guessed the range of your activities or I'd have turned you around there and then! However, the joke is no longer on me. You'll be out of here come the morning or I'll know the reason why. Your car is full of gas, so you have no excuse. I will also contact the car hire firm and arrange to settle your account. This, together with your air fare and over three weeks' free board, should just about cancel this other debt you talk of—if it ever existed!'

'You really mean it?' She was trembling so hard inwardly, she could scarcely speak.

'Sure I mean it!' he flung at her harshly. 'You can take your soft, slender body and easy kisses somewhere else. I suppose that was all part of the act, all with one end in view!' He flung back his handsome head and laughed sarcastically, 'Come to think of it, Miss Sinclair, it might have been interesting to let you stay a while longer. How did you expect you were going to keep me at arms' length? Or were you prepared to even take me into your bed in order to achieve what you wanted? Another few days you might have thought to have me begging.'

As her hand came up, as if to strike him, he caught it, a white ring of cold rage around his mouth. 'Can't you bear to let me go?' he taunted. 'If it's a fond farewell you're after I might as well supply this too.'

Before she quite realised what was happening he jerked her to him again, crushing her against the full length of him until her fair head fell painfully back over his arm. When his mouth came down and brutally assaulted hers she could have cried out, if he had left her with either the breath or inclination to do so. Then, when she thought she was near fainting, she was released, so suddenly she almost fell against the chair behind her. Groping blindly with her hand, she almost collapsed on to it, her legs so weak they wouldn't seem to hold her.

'I'll say goodbye to Oliver for you, so you might avoid the possibility of any harrowing scene. You appear to have a flair for the dramatic, Petronella.'

It might have been some consolation that he didn't call her Miss Sinclair again, but she felt so degraded by his contemptuous indifference of her feelings that all sense deserted her. 'At least,' she choked, 'he asked me to marry him. He acted decently, he didn't insult me.'

Neil flicked her a guarded look, not apparently impressed. The slight, wary narrowing of his glance would be because of Janey. 'Hurd was merely carried away by your too obvious seductiveness and a pair of cloud-grey eyes. Once you're gone he'll soon come to his senses.'

Petra rubbed the back of her hand childishly over her bruised lips. 'You like to rule, don't you?' she couldn't stop herself from crying. 'Other people are merely robots to be directed as you choose. Yet you do it so cleverly no one realises. Oliver has to marry Janey—for your convenience, I suspect, more than his own. You don't even stop to consider if they really love each other.'

'You think that's important, the only reason for marriage?' again he sneered.

'I would hope so.' Irrationally Petra felt it was necessary to pursue this point which was no concern of hers. She felt utterly distracted, but Oliver had been kind. If she could do something for him, then mustn't she try? 'Surely it isn't possible to be happy, to feel really close to someone without being in love?'

'You're quite mistaken.'

'No!'

His voice held a shade of violence which her antagonism didn't appease. 'Don't tell me you aren't aware of other attractions. When I held you in my arms the other night I could have gone much further with you and you couldn't have stopped me. You wouldn't call that love, but could you honestly swear you had no pleasure from it? Every bit of you responded, and I can relive every second of it.'

Her face flushed, painfully red. 'It would take a man like you to put it into words!'

'Seeing I won't get another chance, I see no sense in quibbling. I'd advise you to ask yourself, when you meet a man of Hurd's calibre again, just what it is you really want!'

'If I met Oliver again,' she cried recklessly, 'I would agree to marry him just to spite you!'

His blue eyes were sombre, almost black with derision as they fixed on her white face. 'I believe this would come under the heading of revenge, but as it won't happen I don't intend to worry. Just get out of my sight, girl, at once! The way I feel right now could be dangerous. I won't see you again, but I will arrange to have your car

Take this superb volume
FREE!

Lucy Gillen sets this romance among the wild lochs and mountains of Scotland. **"A Wife for Andrew"** is a touching account of a young governess, her dour yet compassionate employer and the children in his care who suffer at the hands of a jealous woman.

In Betty Neels' **"Fate Is Remarkable"** Sarah's "marriage of convenience" is dramatically altered. Just as Sarah was getting ready to tell Hugo that she'd fallen in love with him, a lovely woman from Hugo's past shows up . . .

In **"Bitter Masquerade"** by Margery Hilton, mistaken identity is the basis of Virginia Dalmont's marriage. When Brent mistook her for her twin sister Anna, she wondered if her love was strong enough to make up for the deceit. . .

In the pages of your FREE GIFT Romance Treasury Volume you'll get to know warm, true-to-life people, and you'll discover the special kind of miracle that love can be. The stories will sweep you to distant lands where intrigue, adventure and the destiny of many lives will thrill you. All three full-length novels are exquisitely bound together in a single hardcover volume that's your FREE GIFT, to introduce you to Harlequin Romance Treasury!

The most beautiful books you've ever seen!
Cover and spine of all volumes feature distinctive gilt designs. And an elegant bound-in ribbon bookmark adds a lovely feminine touch. No detail has been overlooked to make Romance Treasury books as beautiful and lasting as the stories they contain. What a delightful way to enjoy the very best and most popular Harlequin romances again and again!

A whole world of romantic adventures!
If you are delighted with your FREE GIFT volume, you may, if you wish, receive a new Harlequin Romance Treasury volume as published every five weeks or so — delivered right to your door! The beautiful FREE GIFT VOLUME is yours to keep with no obligation to buy anything.

Fill out the coupon today to receive your FREE GIFT VOLUME.

Romance Treasury
from Harlequin

Three exciting, full length Romance novels in one beautiful book ...

THE Romance Treasury Association

FREE gift certificate

Dear Ellen Windsor:

Yes, please send my FREE GIFT VOLUME with no obligation to buy anything. If you do not hear from me after receiving my free gift volume, please mail me the second volume of Romance Treasury. If I decide to keep the second volume, I will pay only $4.97 plus a small charge for shipping and handling (39c). I will then be entitled to examine other volumes at the rate of one volume (3 novels) every five weeks or so, as they are published. Each volume is at the low price of $4.97 plus shipping and handling (39c) and comes to me on a 10-day free approval basis. There is no minimum number of books I must buy. I can stop receiving books at any time simply by notifying you. The FREE GIFT VOLUME is mine to keep forever, no matter what I decide later.

Please Print clearly.   C79-1

_____

Name

_____

Address

_____

City   State / Province   Zip / Postal Code

Romance Treasury

from Harlequin

Offer expires December 31, 1979.

This superb volume is yours
FREE!

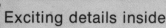

« Exciting details inside

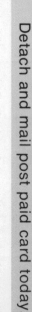

Detach and mail post paid card today.

brought around in the morning, about nine. That should give you plenty of time.'.

It did. Too much, in fact. Petra was ready and waiting, David by her side, long before then. Almost she had been tempted to go earlier and find the car herself, but she was too frightened of running into Neil. Where he was concerned her feeling was too numb even to think about him. To meet him again this morning might unbalance the last of her precarious control devastatingly. She was trying desperately to ignore that she might have fallen in love with him, for what else could account for the almost physical heartache which had torn at her all through the long weary hours of the night? It seemed bitter to realise that if he had lived in a mud hut, without a penny to his name, she would have stayed with him on any terms, but after what she had done and said he would never believe her now.

She hadn't slept, as the dark shadows under her eyes bore witness. Not that she had actually gone to bed. She had sat on the edge of it, her eyes fixed on the distant dark horizon as if hoping inspiration might come with the dawn. As soon as it was light she had packed her few meagre belongings, for long seconds gazing at Neil's pictured face before thrusting the portait deep into the bottom of her bag. She had wanted to leave it, in some way it might have appeased her wounded pride, but at the last moment her resolution failed her and she had been unable to bring herself to part with it.

Then she had to waken David and tell him they were leaving almost immediately. This had been the hardest thing—perhaps after parting from Neil. He had been childishly incredulous, then frankly disbelieving until Petra had began to weep.

It had only been briefly, for she had quickly pulled herself together, but it had been enough to convince him she wasn't joking.

'Oh, Petra!' he'd breathed, his young face almost more bewildered than her own. 'I like it here. Neil and I get along fine. He's shown me such a lot, how to do a lot of things as well.'

'I know, darling.'

David's face, which was tanned and looking so much better than when they had first arrived, crumpled unashamedly, and for a long moment, as Petra put a consoling arm around his shoulder, they clung together.

His voice had trembled slightly, 'I'm going to miss my pony, Petra. I could have gone to school here, I like Canada. I don't think I'd make a good rancher, I'd rather go into something else, but I could have spent my holidays with you and Neil. Didn't you ask him if we could stay? If you're scared to, maybe I . . .'

'No, darling,' Petra had interrupted quickly, unevenly, 'I'm afraid it is not convenient for him to have us.'

'I don't want to go back to London, Petra.'

'I know, but there's nothing else for it.'

'But—those horrid jobs—those men !'

'David !' What had he known about them?

'I'm sorry,' he had mumbled, before her obvious distress, 'I couldn't help noticing. I didn't mean to upset you. I'm not a child, though.'

'Well, you're supposed to be, you're only twelve,' she had said gently, trying rather unsuccessfully to make a little joke out of it. 'I hope you don't mind too much,' she had added helplessly.

He had gazed at her anxiously then. 'Doesn't Neil like you, Petra?'

'Not as much as he likes you, I think.'

'But . . .' Whatever he had been going to say next, the taut expression on Petra's face must have caused him to change his mind. 'Don't worry,' he had assured her quickly, suddenly squaring his thin shoulders, 'I'll look after you.'

She'd been grateful when he had quietly began to pack and, with a tact beyond his tender years, said nothing more.

CHAPTER EIGHT

NEITHER Mrs Cameron or Janey came to bid them good-bye. Petra didn't think either of them were up when she and David went out to wait on the porch, so perhaps they had no idea she was leaving. At breakfast she had told Mrs Allen and seen how the woman had glanced regretfully at David, but she fancied the woman's kindly look hadn't included herself. However, she felt so vulnerably sensitive this morning, she might easily have imagined it.

The car arrived and the driver who brought it was the same young mechanic who had fixed it after her unfortunate accident with the steer. Even now Petra flinched to recall that event, especially when she knew who the tall, mud-coated cowboy had been. It seemed increasingly surprising she hadn't guessed at the time, but then she wasn't particularly bright these days!

She was about to thank the boy as he jumped out of the car when he handed her a package.

'The boss said I was to give you this,' he mumbled, clearly embarrassed by something he didn't altogether understand. 'He said it was something he'd forgotten but that you'd know about it.'

'Yes, I see.' Driving away, after thanking him briefly, Petra passed the package to David. 'I expect you'll find the money there for our return tickets,' she explained dully. 'We——' she had been about to say she wished they didn't have to accept it but hastily decided against it. It would serve no good purpose to disturb David more than was necesssary. He was too pale and very quiet. He looked subdued. When Petra had suggested it he hadn't wanted to go and tell Jake and the boys he was going. She hadn't insisted, realising instinctively he was frightened a momentary weakness might betray him. This sudden departure appeared to be affecting him deeply; better leave him alone.

If he was taking this a lot harder than might have been expected, Petra's heart sank as she thought of what was to come. The bleakness of another bare room again! David had come to really love living on the ranch. How many times, after he had been out with Neil or Jake and the boys, had he related excitedly all his adventures? Just trailing along the creeks with her had filled him with a lively enthusiasm that had been gratifying to see. Even if he wasn't inclined to view ranching or farming as a possible career, he enjoyed being here. He was an intelligent boy; given the right sort of start he might have succeeded in anything he set his mind to.

Now, since leaving the ranch, he looked as if all the enthusiasm had been knocked out of him, and Petra felt directly responsible. If only they could have stayed in the area things might not have seemed so bad. Maybe—her unhappy thoughts whirled distractedly, splintering her consuming numbness—maybe she should have said yes to Oliver's proposal. Wouldn't it have given her everything she needed to take proper care of David? But she wasn't likely to see Oliver again and couldn't possibly seek him out. Or should she? Would it really matter what Neil would think, Janey either, for that matter? Had either of them considered her? No, that probably wasn't fair. She had been the interloper, not them. There were Janey's feelings for Oliver, of course, but this might only amount to infatuation. Hadn't she gone off and left him all those months? Yet Petra's shoulders rose in an unconsciously wry shrug as she drove along. She couldn't possibly, in spite of such a wild flight of fancy, bring herself to call at Oliver's place, so Janey was quite safe.

Firmly she put it from her mind, only to find Neil's callousness of the night before returning to haunt her. But had it really been that? Hadn't she asked for all she'd got? It had been a terrible gamble, coming here, one which hadn't paid off. It was as simple as that. All she could do was try and forget it. Perhaps, all considered, she had escaped lightly. If only she had been able to do more for David!

On the breath of a despairing sigh she heard David saying something about a helicopter.

'We're being followed, Petra,' he cried, twisting his rumpled brown head to see better. 'At least, whoever it is seems to be following the road and keeping a sort of distance.'

'It could be one of the men checking cattle.' Petra dared not take her eyes off the track. She didn't find the dirt road very easy to drive on and was scared of making another mistake like the last. The helicopter could mean a few things. Neil could be making sure they had left, or he might have sent someone to see they got away safely—which could mean much the same thing. Some of the staff had their pilot's licence and used the helicopter for searching out cattle in the bush, but whoever it was up there he was taking his time and this did not seem the object this morning. Sighing again she decided to ignore it and concentrate on the way ahead, praying it would not be long before she reached the main intersection and she could escape on to the highway.

She saw the truck coming towards them a few minutes later while it was still some way off. As the ground was so dry it travelled in the usual dust cloud and it wasn't until it drew nearer that she was startled to see it was Oliver Hurd. Not until then did she remember he had talked of taking them all for a picnic and would like to make an early start. Like Cameron he often used a helicopter, but this morning it had probably been needed elsewhere.

He was almost on top of Petra before he seemed to realise who it was. She saw his mouth almost drop open in surprise. About to pass with a friendly wave, she was forced to stop as he swerved dangerously, nearly bumping into them. He didn't attempt to ease his way past but, after another keen glance, to ensure he wasn't having hallucinations, he switched off his ignition and scrambled down to her.

'Petra!' he exclaimed, frowning. 'What on earth are you doing here?'

'I'm sorry, Oliver.' She changed into neutral and put a

foot on the brake, but this was all. She had no desire to waste time over useless explanations. 'We can't stop and talk, Oliver, we're in a hurry.'

'You're leaving?'

'It looks like it,' she smiled briefly.

'Petra!'

Oliver's voice was suddenly so urgent she had to stop him. Somehow she sensed what was coming and wished to spare him the humiliation of being refused twice. She could never marry him, not after knowing Neil. He had spoilt her for any other men.

'Please!' she entreated him sharply, before turning hurriedly to David. 'Just wait a second, David,' she said, 'I just want a word with Oliver.'

Quickly she jumped out to join him, brushing her long hair from out of her eyes as the light breeze caught it. David mustn't hear. It might sound too much like a betrayal, denying David a second chance, but she knew she couldn't ever belong to Oliver now.

Yet, for a moment, he was very persuasive. Staring at her hot, unhappy face, he accused her loudly, 'You never told me!'

'We only decided this morning, in rather a hurry.'

He frowned, not so easily deceived as she'd hoped. 'Where are you going?'

'Back home, to England.'

'Petra,' he began hoarsely, his voice so full of pleading she had to steel herself. 'Darling ...'

Then suddenly, before he could continue, there was the whirr of the forgotten helicopter above them, and the noise of its landing was so deafening that further speech was impossible.

'What the devil!' Oliver's eyes, narrowing to slits against the sun, showed angry surprise. 'Oh,' he shouted, just as the powerful engine purred into silence, 'it's only Neil!'

Neil it was, and though her heart pounded with shock, Petra only stared at him dully. Had he come to wish David and her a belated goodbye? He had said, last night, he wouldn't see them again, but he must have changed his mind.

Oliver's gaze was sullen as Neil approach them. He looked tall and virile, certainly as if he had enjoyed a good night's sleep, Petra thought bitterly. After that first swift impression she found she couldn't look at his face. As he strode up to them she kept her eyes glued to the road, praying it would not be many minutes before both men were gone.

After one brief nod Neil ignored Oliver. His eyes were on Petra and, although she didn't look at him, she could almost feel their sharp impact. 'I want you to come with me, Petronella,' he commanded coolly, confounding her impression that he had merely dropped down to say farewell, or remind her of another sin she had forgotten. His usual slow drawl was gone and he sounded very decisive—so much so that Petra couldn't now stop herself from staring at him, searching for words of refusal which wouldn't come. But, as if curiously struck dumb, she made no move towards the helicopter, which must surely indicate her desire to remain where she was.

Before Oliver, either, could voice any verbal protest, Neil instructed him curtly, 'You can take David back to the ranch with you in your truck. Janey is waiting, she mentioned that you're going on a picnic. Mrs Allen has promised to keep an eye on David until his sister and I return. I'm afraid there's been a slight misunderstanding.'

Carelessly, as if he had merely been discussing the weather, he turned and bent his head to the car window on David's side, speaking to him in a low voice Petra couldn't hear. Whatever it was she couldn't account for the expression of dawning delight which spread across David's freckled, anxious features, nor did she catch his whispered reply.

Coming out of her brief trance, she only knew it was about time she put an end to such nonsense. If Neil was intent on prolonging the agony of parting then she must refuse to go along with it. Oliver, to her amazement, as if he recognised in Neil a stronger personality, made no further objection but proceeded towards his truck, obviously expecting David to follow.

'Don't!' Petra called, making a dive for her car door. Angrily she glanced at Neil. 'I'm not coming with you, Neil Cameron, I think we've talked enough!'

David, taking advantage of the fact that Neil whipped immediately to Petra's side, scurried after Oliver like a rabbit.

'David!' she cried, panic-stricken, but he didn't hear her—or pretended not to.

'Come on!' As Petra stared helplessly after the fast disappearing station wagon, she felt herself almost lifted across the grass into the helicopter. Then they were in the air, scattering a shower of birds, Neil looking as if it was all in the day's work.

The small red car was still at the side of the road, and she heard him calling the ranch, telling Jake to send a man to collect it. His package, along with her handbag, he had taken from the back seat as he'd talked to David. These he dropped on her lap, taking no notice when she sullenly thrust them away.

She had no idea where he was taking her. She felt so churned up inside that, to begin with anyway, everything out the windows dissolved into a misty blur. Even to look at Neil was enough to make her shudder, as she began apprehensively to realise just how much she really cared for him. If she had hoped it was just imagination, to see him again was to be forced to acknowledge the truth. She didn't know what she was going to do about it, but right at that moment she didn't seem to care. Everything, these last few minutes, had happened so quickly, she couldn't seem to take in that any of it was real. She had an odd inclination to both laugh and cry and it took every bit of her dwindling control to do neither.

His hands were sure and strong on the controls and while she knew he was an excellent pilot, today he seemed preoccupied, as if his mind was not wholly on the job. It couldn't be on her, either, Petra hazarded, as he hadn't

addressed a word to her since they had left the ground.
Nor had he looked at her after assuring himself she was
safely seated.

Blindly she turned again to the window, this time con-
centrating. They were leaving the flat, rolling prairie,
skimming the foothills, and beyond these she could see the
mountains. She had never flown here before and found
she had a superb view of the high peaks with their abrupt
slopes and irregular surfaces, many of which were cut deep
with canyons and ravines. It was the eastern side of the
Rockies and Alberta was world-famous for its mountain
scenery. The mountains stretched, she knew, in many
places over a hundred miles wide with many of the peaks
ranging over twelve and thirteen thousand feet high,
Mount Logan in the Yukon being four thousand feet
higher than Mont Blanc in the Alps.

Like a sleepwalker she began counting the many small
lakes which carried their reflection and felt faintly put
out when Neil came down by one of them. They had it
all to themselves, it was like being in a beautiful wilderness
and even though Petra was getting used to such magnificent scenery she never failed to be startled by it. It always
appeared to her like a veritable paradise, or could have
been, she thought ruefully, if she hadn't known a man
called Cameron!

Scarcely able to bring herself to do so, she turned her
fair head to see what he was doing. He was too familiar
with the terrain to be admiring it as she was doing. He
talked about fishing, easily catching a dozen trout before
breakfast, about riding and hunting, camping out just for
pleasure but, like any native, she doubted if he ever saw
it through a visitor's incredulous, appreciative eyes.

Now, as she suspected, his eyes were not on the sur-
rounding countryside. They were on her, narrowly, as if
he was still trying to make up his mind about something.
Whatever was on his mind, Petra decided, must have got
there in a hurry. That was if it concerned her, which
seemed likely. Last night he had had everything cut and
dried, he had only wanted to be rid of her. Whatever

accounted for this change of front, if this was what this was, escaped her imagination.

She didn't fool herself, however, that he was very kindly disposed towards her. The face he surveyed her from was still hard, lacking any remorseful tenderness which might have brought a thread of reassurance, yet when he spoke there was no hint of his former harshness in his voice.

'You'd better get down,' he said, 'and we'll sit by the lake. It will be pleasanter than staying in here.'

When she made no attempt to move his glance sharpened and he slid lightly from his door to move around to hers. 'Here,' he held up his arms obligingly, 'let me help you. You look a little stunned.'

Not knowing what else to do, she lifted her hands like a child, placing them on his broad shoulders, obeying as if without a will of her own. When he lifted her on to the ground it seemed to heave momentarily beneath her feet, but this was all. 'Thank you,' she breathed unevenly, her gaze managing no further than his chin.

As his hands released their grip on her narrow waist she felt a tremor run through her and turned swiftly from him to find a patch of soft grass. Not wanting to look at him again right away, she stared about her, noticing the tall ponderosa pines and how the silver willow dipped to the pale green water. Her eyes strayed towards the wave-washed pebbles on the shore and moved on, across the wind-rippled surface, to the rocks which formed part of the mountain wall at the other side of the lake.

Piles of driftwood lay twisted and wrinkled about them, dry as tinder from the heat of the sun. Neil piled a heap of it and, her eyes drawn back to him dully, Petra watched him take a match from his pocket and apply a flame.

'It isn't really cold, but we're high up and the air is fresh off the water. A fire is cheerful,' he smiled grimly, as if nothing else came into this category.

Petra tried, but she couldn't manage to return his smile, if that was what it was, but she did feel slightly better because of the fire. As it crackled and blazed it was something she could pretend to be absorbed in, and it provided an excuse not to look at her tormentor.

He sat down about a couple of feet from her, on a log. 'I brought you up here,' he said, looking down on her, 'because I wanted you away from the ranch, where you won't be influenced by atmosphere, if you like.'

'We talked last night,' she returned stiffly. 'I can't think there's anything left to say.'

His eyes grew darker at her careless tones and he retorted with what seemed an effort. 'Quite a lot, now that I've had time to think things over. You must admit you did rather spring things on me?'

Somehow she couldn't go along with this opinion. 'You don't seem a man easily surprised by anything. I've always imagined you take most things in your stride.'

'Most things,' he agreed suavely, 'but blackmail is a bit out of the ordinary. It takes some time to come to terms with it—almost more than I could swallow.'

'Blackmail!' she exclaimed incredulously.

'Petronella!' His own exclamation was softer, if more deadly, as he noticed her indignant colour. 'You threatened to tell my neighbours unless I paid up. What else would you call that?'

'I remember,' she stammered in confusion, 'but it wasn't really like that, as you must know. I'm not after money! All I want is a settled home for David.'

'And if I don't give him one you're having to consider who else will?'

It was then, as she shot a startled glance at his taut face, that she realised what this was all about. At least she thought she did. This morning, after she had gone, it had suddenly come to him that she might easily bump into Oliver. It was not beyond contemplating that he might just as easily have visualised her calling at Oliver's home to beg for shelter. Janey would naturally have told him about the picnic and he had simply put two and two together and chased after her. He was either very fond of Janey or determined to get rid of her and was not going to allow Petra to upset his plans. Rather than do this he would offer Petra a home until the danger was over. Not, of course, that he had offered yet, she could be vastly mistaken in her wild conclusions.

Maybe she wasn't being fair. He wanted the best for his stepsister and wouldn't see her heart broken, which might be the natural conclusion if Oliver went off with another girl. Petra could have laughed if she hadn't felt so miserable. Didn't Neil have any idea how she felt about him? Didn't he realise she could never marry Oliver Hurd, nor ask him for asylum, even if he hadn't lived on Neil's doorstep—fifty miles being considered just that, in this country!

Not sure how to tell Neil this, Petra hesitated, her hurt pride making it far from easy to put it into words. What excuse could she offer for not accepting Oliver's proposal? How could she confess it was because she loved another man? Neil would guess. Hadn't he held her in his arms? He had known how deeply she had responded. One hint that she wasn't interested in Oliver and the game would be up. Neil was so many years older and wiser. He was too astute.

'Petronella!' he was prompting, tersely impatient when she didn't speak. 'I asked you a question, and I'm having to guess the answer. I'm going to ask another and this time I want a straight reply, not a lot of anxious sighing! What was Oliver saying to you with that look on his face?'

'Nothing.' In spite of the warning just issued, Petra hung her head stubbornly. He couldn't physically wring it out of her and he had no right to know the answer to —some things!

Before she could continue he bit off contemptuously, 'Okay, Petronella, you don't have to put yourself out. Some things I can read quite plainly on your face. Suppose we leave Oliver for a few minutes and I'll tell you what I propose?'

Unbidden, David's expression, as she had last seen it beside the car, came back to her. 'David looked so happy!' Antagonism burst into speech. 'I can't think what you told him, but if you said he could stay then I think you're cruel !'

'Hush!' he commanded sharply 'Just listen. You want him to have a good education?'

'A good home as much as anything,' she protested wearily.

'If he could have both, how grateful would you be?'

Gratitude? A wave of apprehension widened her smoky grey eyes. He had never mentioned such a thing before. It could mean anything. She wasn't exactly a fool!

'Not what you're thinking, not yet anyway,' he assured her cryptically. 'I need someone at the ranch and you could be useful. Manna from heaven, maybe, only I didn't realise it until this morning.'

'How could I be useful?' she asked carefully, trying to steady her thudding heart. It was amazing the effect this man had on her. To think of being near him again, every day, was almost enough to make her feel dizzy.

Just as carefully he watched her. 'Mrs Allen's leaving. It's been on the cards for some time, events recently have merely precipitated it a little. She's getting on and her brother, whose wife has died recently in New York, wants her to join him. So it follows I'll need a new housekeeper.'

Never in a thousand years had Petra expected this. Nor had she ever seen herself as a housekeeper, although she was fully conversant with their duties as they had always had one at Redwell. Slightly stunned, she asked tentatively, 'How about Mrs Cameron? Won't she mind?'

He shook his dark head solemnly. 'No—for many reasons, but I'll confine myself to two. Fay isn't interested in anything domestic and she can't abide the ranch since my father died.'

'There's still Janey.'

'Ah, yes, Janey.' His mouth twisted. 'I would never allow her to become entrenched in such a position. This is where I shall expect you to really put yourself out. I want her married to Oliver. Think you could face up to that?' he sneered.

'I don't know ...' Petra was aware of his narrowed eyes on her hot cheeks and wished she felt free to tell him she would help every way she could to do as he asked, and with pleasure, as she felt sure Janey and Oliver were right for each other. But if Neil was assured that she thought like this mightn't he have second thoughts about asking her to stay? Wasn't it because he was afraid she might pinch Oliver from under Janey's nose that he was so magnanimously offering her a job and a home? It was quite clear that he felt duty bound to have her where he could keep an eye on her. For David's sake she must swallow her pride, the last bit she seemed to have left, and pretend she wouldn't mind being Neil Cameron's slave, even to being treated like a doormat! Having to see Neil every day, feeling as she did about him, might be the biggest hurdle, but not insurmountable, if she put her mind to it.

'Well, what conclusions have you come to, Miss Sinclair?'

Doubtfully she glanced up at him. 'If you think I can do it?'

'Come on,' visibly his strong shoulder muscles appeared to relax, 'where's all that warlike confidence? Mrs Allen won't leave until the end of the week and is willing to show you the ropes. The widow of one of our stockmen is still with us and comes in every day, as you know. The other wives help when we want them.'

'Seems like I'll just need to sit on a stool and give orders,' she returned, deliberately flippant.

'Don't delude yourself, Petronella. You'll do more than that.'

'And—in exchange?'

'I'll keep you, clothe you and send David to a good school. Afterwards to my old college, if he makes the grade.'

That sounded ominous! If they both made the grade, he probably meant. Long years of domestic servitude stretched endlessly before her. Not that she would have minded this if Neil had loved her, but, under the present circumstances, could she ever stick it out? How could she bear such a sort of closely distant relationship? 'I won't be able to repay you,' she mumbled, staring away from him.

'I thought it was I who was in your debt. I distinctly recall your saying so,' he taunted.

'I remember,' her head drooped as she bit her lip sharply. 'It was what I'd been led to believe, but I realise that I haven't a strong case.'

'No case whatsoever, Petronella, and I'm glad you acknowledge it. I have no wish to live with constant re-criminations.'

It was times like this when she hated him. Keeping her head lowered so he wouldn't see the angry sparkle in her eyes, she tried to speak levelly. 'How about your family? Janey might accept me, but are you sure Mrs Cameron will?'

'Just help Janey get married,' he assured her coolly, 'and I think you'll find no one will mind a thing.'

'What if Janey minds being pushed around?' Petra persisted, not altogether convinced. Neil's whole attitude towards both Janey and her mother she found confusing.

'So long as you push her in Oliver's direction, she'll have no objections,' he replied. 'She'll get much more out of a husband than she gets out of me, and I'm not exactly un-generous.'

He really did want poor Janey off his hands! After this was accomplished to his satisfaction, would it be her turn? Mightn't he be planning even now to get rid of her as easily as Janey?

About to question him more closely, Petra suddenly found herself unable to utter another word. She started to shake as everything that had happened over the past few weeks began catching up on her. A strange trembling attacked her limbs which she couldn't stop or seem to hide. There was a frightening feeling that she was going to pass out and there was nothing she could do about it. 'Neil!' she breathed, her eyes mutely appealing in the deathly whiteness of her face.

She knew nothing of Neil dropping down on his knees and catching her as she slumped over, of putting strong arms around her shuddering body and drawing her close.

She only knew that the effort it cost not to slip completely into an enticing oblivion was an almost physical pain.

While she longed for a few comforting words, the ones he spoke were far from that. 'Is this because of David or Oliver?' he asked tersely. Then, when she couldn't reply, 'One of the first lessons in growing up, Petronella, is to learn that we can't always have things our own way. I've agreed to everything you want regarding David, so I guess it's not him.'

A half hysterical sob rose to Petra's tight throat which she could barely suppress. Neil must think what he liked! Through a thick haze she realised that if she was to stay at the ranch it was better that he should believe she cared for some other man. Otherwise he might suspect where her feelings really lay. Not that she knew now whether she loved Neil or not. How could she possibly love a man so lacking in sensitivity that he didn't hesitate to deride her, even when she felt ill! If he imagined she was merely pining after Oliver, well, let him!

'Petronella!' As if her shivering body alarmed and disturbed him, his arms tightened. 'You know this will pass. Oliver would never have made you happy. Besides, you couldn't respond to other men the way you do if you loved him.'

For a long moment indignation warred with shock as she understood the implications of what he had said. He couldn't possibly have guessed! If she could find the strength she must deny it and push him away ... 'I don't know what you're talking about,' she whispered, on another dry sob, which seemed to prevent her somehow from escaping.

'You don't?' Careless of her shivering disability, or taking advantage of it, he pushed the heavy hair back from her hot forehead. His hand touched the creamy skin of her cheek and slid around under her chin, lifting her mouth to his slowly descending one. 'This could prove the best antidote for a lot of the troubles which beset you, as well as answering your naïve question,' he murmured.

If she had wanted his tenderness she wasn't to get it.

The swift kisses he pressed on her quivering mouth were like a prelude to much wilder music. He seemed intent on tasting the glittering tears which fell from her suddenly drenched eyes and trickled their way into his mouth. There was something faintly sensuous about the way he traced them down her cheek, the way his fingers eased the slight tension around her lips, gently forcing them apart. Then his mouth closed on hers with a small exclamation of possession and the desire to fight him left her.

After the first minute her mouth began to open on its own accord as great swirls of sensation began to multiply and consume her. Feeling her vulnerable response, he lifted her completely into his arms, holding her trembling body to him, exploring her mouth with a driving masculinity until the cascade of feeling between them mounted inexorably.

All need to escape him, to hate him, rapidly dissolved into a molten, tempestuous urgency to get as near to him as possible. He was holding her with passion and enough violence to make the blood pound in her ears. It was frightening the delight he gave her as he half turned, pinning her beneath him, his hand sliding under her thin shirt to close over the full curve of her breast without seeking permission or offering apology.

'Don't try to fight it!' she heard him mutter thickly against her bruised lips. 'Remember we have a ghost to exorcise.'

She felt bound and helpless, almost drugged with sensation, not able to think as she lay, a not unwilling prisoner in his arms. Did he mean Oliver or those other men—how could he imagine they involved her thoughts now? Unable to stop herself, she arched shamelessly against him, gripped in a kind of nervous, shaking intensity as he eased the weight of his heavy body slightly, allowing his hands to caress her fully. She lay rapt, her skin burning to his touch but finding it irresistible. Her heart raced under his moving hand and there was nothing she could do or wanted to do to stop it. Her arms gripped his broad shoulders and then crossed behind his neck and, unbidden, her mouth moved against his as if trying to transmit her unsatisfied yearning. It was frightening and spellbinding, the way he seemed quite literally to possess her without actually doing a thing. It was devastating, a breathless devouring excitement which must surely arrive at its own natural conclusion.

Seconds later she felt cheated, consumed by frustration when he lifted his strong head and put her gently from him. Her hair danced in silken disarray about her flushed cheeks, brushing across the stormy longing in her grey eyes. Oddly, as her heavy lashes lifted, she felt bereft of words.

'Neil?' she whispered, as if begging for a logical explanation as to why the magic which had caught them up in whirling wings couldn't continue.

'I might never have let you escape,' he looked at her so coolly she felt a sting of humiliation, 'but the purpose of this exercise wasn't to see how far I could go. You were on the verge of hysteria and it sometimes takes one shock to combat another. Do you feel better now?'

Better! How could he ask it? 'No,' she said sullenly, her face mirroring all too clearly her thoughts. They were still close, even if he held her at arms' length. Surely he couldn't pretend to be indifferent? 'Neil?' Blindly she inched nearer, uncaring that he might think her without modesty, as she reached out to him.

He was one step ahead of her as usual. 'Petronella,' he exclaimed sternly, thrusting away her groping hands, disallowing her ragged breathing, 'this is what I meant when I said you were too vulnerable where men are concerned. You have to grow up.'

This really did bring Petra to her senses. She couldn't think of a more beastly thing he might have said. Did he truly believe she responded like this to every man who looked her way? If so, she was better off without him. She shrank back from him as if suddenly stung, yet she could only think to say, 'I'm not a child!'

He paled, as if for one indiscreet moment he would have liked to agree. 'We'll argue about that another day,' he smiled soberly, jumping suddenly to his feet. 'I have a basket in the helicopter with some food and coffee. If you have something before we go you'll soon feel yourself.'

Before he came back she made a valiant effort to pull herself completely together, and must have partly succeeded as Neil seemed to relax when he returned with the basket and looked at her.

'How did you know you were going to need it?' she asked, striving to maintain an appearance of normality.

'I didn't,' he shrugged, setting out cups and uncorking a flask. 'I had intended spending the day in the high country and Mrs Allen had this ready for me.'

'But you didn't go, to the high country, I mean?'

He tossed her an sandwich which she guessed had never been designed for a lady. 'I guess something made me change my mind, but we'll leave it for now. When a man isn't sure he's acting wisely it can rankle.'

With Neil Cameron it would. She had never met a man so sure of himself. Yet only a little bit of it, she conceded, was arrogance. His was the kind of assurance other people relied on. The kind to make a woman feel cherished and protected. Her father had had it, if not nearly to such a degree. No doubt, she thought, her mind winging back to Neil, Janey was the reason for Neil's uncommon confusion and Petra would be unwise to insist on further discussion. It could be pushing her luck too far. He had seen Janey's future happiness endangered and rushed to her rescue. It was as simple as that. 'Thank you, Cameron,' she murmured, absently accepting a mug of steaming coffee.

'That's another thing,' he took up crisply, as when their fingers inevitably touched her eyes flew compulsively to his face.

'What?' she whispered, feeling tautly disturbed again.

'I want no more Camerons. From now on it has to be Neil.'

When he issued an order like that there was nothing she could do about it. 'If you say so—Neil.'

'There,' his glance was studied, 'no worse than having a tooth pulled out.'

What did he know about that, with his perfect set! 'I'll

feel like a stranger. It came with your portrait. We all called you Cameron.'

'It might not be a bad thing to begin all over again, then.'

'I'm not sure I would want that!' she choked fervently on a crumb, but the sandwiches and coffee were having a beneficial effect. They even gave her the strength to attack him coldly. 'I think it was criminal of you not to introduce yourself straight away. I could be excused, with all that mud on your face, but I don't know why you did it.'

He glanced at her rather grimly. 'I don't know myself exactly. I never thought to see the day when a mere girl would get under my skin to the extent of making me act very much out of character. I suspect Jake is still trying to figure it out.'

'Perhaps it was a touch of the sun?'

'Maybe.' He was narrowly non-committal as he watched the neat pile of sandwiches disappearing. 'When did you last eat, Petronella?' he drawled.

Not until then did she realise he had contented himself with coffee and she hastily pushed the last of the food towards him. 'Oh, I'm sorry,' she said hastily, her cheeks pink.

'Did you have any breakfast?'

'No. I wasn't hungry.'

'I noticed myself you ate very little at dinner last night. Did you sleep?' he asked smoothly, his eyes sharply on her.

'No ...'

'I thought not.' The dark blue of his eyes glittered. 'But I'd advise you in future to mend your ways. If you intend being much use to me, Petronella!'

CHAPTER NINE

ALL the way back to the ranch Petra wondered if she was doing the right thing, and the next few days were to bring no clear answer. It seemed ironical that having reached the goal she had set out to achieve, she should be so filled with apprehension for the future. Hiding her real feelings for Neil Cameron would be difficult enough, but the thought suddenly struck her that he might one day get married. While she didn't dare ask him about this, Janey had mentioned he had several close women friends. A man like Neil Cameron would! Didn't it follow, then, that he would eventually ask one of them to come and share his life, here at the ranch?

Petra felt a wave of desolation strike into her cruelly. It might be isolated, sometimes even frugal, but a more wonderful existence she could scarcely envisage, now that she had come to love it almost as much as she did its owner. Any woman might jump at the chance of marrying Neil Cameron, but wouldn't it take a very special person? There might be no shortage of money, but that seemed only of secondary inmportance here. Here an ability to adapt to quite a lonely environment, a basic love of country things would take precedence over most everything else. It was one thing to consider Neil's marriage logically in her mind but quite another to subdue the increasing clamour of her own hungry body. She must stay because, at the moment, she had no other option, but she could make sure that when the time came for Neil to take a bride she was in a position to take herself off elsewhere.

At the ranch no one seemed surprised to see her back, which made Petra wonder if anyone apart from Mrs Allen had known anything about her going away. That David was completely happy with the new arrangements seemed the thing which really mattered. In retrospect the whole incident of their leaving, including the interlude in Neil's arms, which he had meant to be comforting, was terrifying, but she would almost be willing to do it again to see the delight in David's face when she had told him her news. Ignoring her doubts, she assured him the arrangement was permanent, at least until he had finished his education, and was rewarded with a warm hug.

Petra, ashamed that she might have led him to believe she had gained a kind of major victory, said, 'You realise Neil doesn't really owe us a thing, so we should be grateful?' She went on to tell him about Mrs Allen leaving. 'I'm going to take over her duties, David, but this will never be enough to cover the cost of everything. I don't see how we'll ever be able to repay, but one day we might have an opportunity.'

Which sounded horribly vague, but it was the best she could do.

David didn't seem at all daunted by the idea of boarding school, not even when it was now almost a reality. 'I know it might be tough to begin with, Petra, and I'm going to miss you, but I'll be twelve, and once I get used to it, it'll be fun. You see, I'm going to need this education if I'm going to do all the things I want to. Dad told me how it was at school with him and Neil enjoyed it too. Neil has explained a whole lot. He sure is a nice guy, Petra!'

Wryly she winced. David picked it all up from the boys, but while it came naturally from them, David's often exaggerated enunciation sounded amusing. But she got used to it and as he grew up his enthusiasm for a new vocabulary would surely calm down. For the moment he had transferred his attention to a pair of old sixguns which he wore stuck realistically in a gunbelt. Neil had assured her mildly that he was sure this wouldn't pave the way for future violence.

Mrs Allen, Petra decided, was too keen to get away to bother herself with what had happened between Neil and Petra. She seemed intent on leaving and was looking forward to New York. Maybe because of this she was more communicative than she had been since Petra had arrived and was quite willing to explain where everything was kept. She even went so far as to show Petra around the house, which the girl supposed she would have done with whoever had been taking over. Everything was more or less as Petra had expected. It was large and rambling with numerous bedrooms besides her own leading off the long, white corridor upstairs. Neil's own room gave Petra a jolt, although she had stiffened herself against it as Mrs Allen had opened the door. His bed was still unmade, the imprint of his head still on the pillow, his bedcovers in a tumbled heap, almost on the floor, as if they had been thrown impatiently aside when he had got up. She had stood numbly, a curious weakness invading her limbs while Mrs Allen crossly clicked her tongue as she picked things up. At the same time she had remarked that Neil's room was not normally like this, and, while he liked his bed made, on no account did he approve of anyone invading his privacy afterwards. Petra's face had grown hot as she neatly folded his pyjama trousers, as instructed. There was no sign of any top. When she had asked, Mrs Allen had said shortly he didn't wear any. It was only then that Petra recognised suffocatingly that there might be certain aspects to her new job which she'd never considered. Mrs Allen, she was glad to note, hadn't seemed to see her burning cheeks, but then she wasn't in the mood to notice anything. She seemed only too relieved that Neil had found someone so quickly and was quite prepared to think Petra very suitable, being his cousin.

As Neil had predicted, his stepmother made little demur when she learnt of Petra's new role, but as she had been heard to say she disapproved of vague relations being kept in idleness perhaps this was not surprising. So far as it went, Petra's gratitude towards the woman was shortlived as Mrs Cameron appeared to think she was here to order at will. And as for Neil himself, while he treated her civilly in the presence of others, he made no great secret of the fact that she was no longer a guest in his house. Yet his attitude stiffened her backbone as nothing else might have done. When Janey pointed out sharply that some of the stockmen's wives might have managed as well as she was doing, Petra decided she would show them, even if she worked her fingers to the bone!

This didn't actually come to pass for, as Janey had pointed out, she did have plenty of help. She did try, however, to impress, maybe more than she might otherwise have done. She had persevered with French cookery at school, after discovering she had a natural talent for it, and afterwards, at Redwell, when her father had entertained, she had occasionally produced some exotic dishes which earned unstinting praise. Here, alas, she soon realised that her attempt to make an impression had misfired. Oliver, arriving on the first evening after Mrs Allen's departure, was so generous with his appreciation that he scarcely took his eyes off her, and Janey looked mortally offended.

'Not the most brilliant of moves!' Neil said dryly, as he invaded the kitchen after dinner.

Unhappily Petra didn't have to ask him to explain, although she privately decided a lot of things might be better left unsaid. 'How was I to know?' she retorted vaguely. She didn't want to enter into another argument about Oliver. Inside she felt more than a little exhausted, the last few days seeming to have been even more of a strain than those which had preceded them.

Neil didn't hesitate about not sparing her. 'We have an agreement, Petra.'

'I haven't forgotten.'

'You could have fooled me!'

Stung, she retorted, 'You make it sound as if it was something I'd done deliberately!'

'Just so long as it was unintentional, but don't let it happen again. This conversation might seem crazy, but Oliver is very susceptible. When Oliver is around you stick to a plain roast. A waterlogged vegetable could be a good idea. There might be no limits to your imagination —for the time being.'

'You're impossible!' she flared, not liking the sardonic

glitter in his eyes. 'Just so long as you confine your own imagination I'll do very well!'

'It didn't take a lot of that to read what was in Oliver's eyes this evening,' he jeered.

For a taut moment her wide indignant eyes fell from his to flicker down on her crumpled skirt and blouse which she had worn for weeks. 'Do you honestly think I could attract anyone in this?' she cried impulsively.

'So already you're grumbling, throwing out hints, unsatisfied with your lot!'

'Oh!' Furiously she flung away from him, but she managed only one step before he caught her, drawing her back.

'I like my servants to face me when I'm speaking to them,' he spoke coolly in her ear.

'Why, you ...!'

'Petronella!'

'Oh, all right. I'm sorry!' Even his arms loosely around her were having an odd effect, not one she particularly welcomed as she felt painful nerves tightening all over her body.

'That's better, if singularly lacking in enthusiasm,' he grinned indifferently down on her as he turned her neatly around, teasing her too obvious attempts to control her temper. 'I think if Oliver persists I must be willing to assist more myself. Like this, for instance.'

There was a sound, which he had obviously heard, outside the door, and with startled eyes she noticed Oliver opening it, Janey behind him, the coffee tray in her hands. Then Neil's bent head blotted everything out.

Seconds later he was surveying her firmly kissed lips, noting their satisfactory trembling. 'We must see what we can do about your wardrobe,' he murmured, examining her very thoroughly. 'Tomorrow we'll go to town.'

There was the sound of someone turning abruptly and footsteps fading. 'Did you need to do that?' Petra hissed, ignoring what he said about town. 'Don't you think it was slightly ridiculous?'

'You might not believe it, Petra,' he drawled, 'but I'm

ready to grasp at any excuse. Something you might do well to remember when you try me too far.'

Mrs Cameron came to her room later that night, her face more than a little unfriendly. 'Janey has been telling me she saw you and Neil in the kitchen,' she began without preamble.

Petra felt her cheeks flame red and she thought guilt must be written all over her. What sort of a story had Janey related? 'He was simply asking to have his breakfast half an hour earlier,' she hedged. For the most part this was the truth, as he had requested it as he had left her. So that he could be available to take her to town—whether or not she was agreeable.

Mrs Cameron was not so easily put off. 'Janey hinted that he had you in his arms.'

The heat in Petra's cheeks didn't subside and her heart sank before Mrs Cameron's obvious antagonism. 'It was a mistake,' she insisted, 'as you must very well know. Neil was—he was only teasing.' How she wished she could have told Mrs Cameron that he had been merely doing it for Janey's sake, but it was too much to expect Mrs Cameron to believe that Oliver could be attracted to another girl when Janey was around. It would be like adding insult to injury!

'Why should he want to consult you?' Mrs Cameron seemed deliberately insistent, her officious manner plainly indicating that she was far from satisfied with Petra's brief explanation.

'I am his housekeeper.' Petra tried to stare at Mrs Cameron with dignity, trying not to think how her words seemed to hang rather meaninglessly between them.

Quite obviously Mrs Cameron wasn't impressed either. 'We all know what that means!' she retorted coldly, a spiteful curl to her thin lips.

Petra went white. 'Please, Mrs Cameron, I'm only trying to be useful. I thought you approved.'

Mrs Cameron, now she was getting into her stride, had no pity for naïve little girls who had no business to look as beautiful as Petra. Since her husband had died she had had no one to slay with her odd bouts of vindictiveness. Neil wouldn't stand for it and Janey, for all her meek demeanour, would only stand for so much. Angrily she ignored Petra's halting explanation. 'What will you do,' she wanted to know, 'after Janey is married and I've gone back to the city? Even your brother will be away at school.'

'I expect to stay here.' Petra's firmness faltered as she realised, with an agony of confusion, just what Mrs Cameron was getting at.

'You and Neil, alone!'

'Mrs Cameron, please!' The sudden fury which shook Petra caused her to shake, yet subsided almost as quickly. Might her position here not seem as odd to others as it apparently did to Mrs Cameron? She chewed nervously on her full bottom lip, aware of the other woman's smirking sneer and not wishing to incite her further. 'Mrs Edwards, the stockman's widow, will probably be living in by then,' she offered, without that much conviction.

'I know nicely who Mrs Edwards is.' Mrs Cameron spoke icily. 'She's a respectable and very capable middle-aged woman, verging on the elderly. She makes the point of your being here more than slightly ridiculous, especially when she might have been tailor-made for your job.'

'I don't see,' Petra began desperately, feeling more like some small trapped animal by the minute, 'any point in continuing this discussion. You don't understand!'

'Just so long as you do!' Mrs Cameron hesitated, then swept past Petra to the door. Obviously she would have liked to have said more and perhaps only the thought of Neil's possible wrath stopped her. She turned, her pale eyes hard, choosing her words with cool care. 'You mustn't get me wrong, my dear. I would feel responsible if anything happened to you. Men are only too keen to avail themselves of something handed them on a plate, and Neil is no exception!'

Bitterly, feeling decidedly distraught, Petra stared at the closed door for minutes after Mrs Cameron had gone. Was it ever wise to imagine one's troubles over? She might, she realised, have been a stupid little fool about a lot of things, but wasn't it too late to back out now? She must brace herself to sit out Fay's loaded vindictiveness, if this was all that it was.

Petra was honest enough to admit to herself that Mrs Cameron was probably justified in thinking some of the things she did. And mightn't she be as aware as Neil of Oliver's admiring glances in Petra's direction? The woman was doing nothing out of the ordinary in defending her ewe lamb. There must be something about Janey to arouse such protectiveness; even Neil seemed prepared to go to any lengths on her behalf. Nevertheless, neither Mrs Cameron nor Janey would be keen to challenge Neil outright, and no matter what their suspicions they had no case as yet. Before they were gone, thus depriving her of the chaperon-age Mrs Cameron now appeared to consider necessary, something might be arranged to Mrs Cameron's satisfaction. In the meantime she must make sure she didn't pro-voke Neil into any further forms of retaliation. Clearly he had only intended demonstrating to Oliver that Petra was willing to flirt with every available male. If she was honour bound not to deny such an impression, surely she didn't have to actively foster it! Neil could go and amuse himself elsewhere, she decided bleakly.

It seemed the middle of the night when she arrived next morning in the kitchen. Neil was drinking coffee by the stove. Everyone called it the stove, but in reality it was a beautiful shining electric cooker. It was arrayed side by side with a dishwasher and every other gleaming piece of equipment one could possibly wish for. Not even the most modern of kitchens could boast of more. The only con-cession here was the huge scrubbed table which occupied a lot of the floor and which Petra imagined might com-fortably accommodate every man on the ranch, if need be.

Neil didn't move as he watched Petra stumble towards him across the linoleum-covered floor. 'Hello, house-keeper!' he jeered softly. 'What sort of time do you call this?'

'It's not yet five!' She glared at him because in a pair of close-fitting jeans that showed the length of his powerful limbs he was enough to take a girl's breath away. His shirt was checked and open at the neck and she was annoyed that she couldn't match his casual elegance, not even at this hour of the day. Her thin T-shirt had a coffee stain down one side and she hadn't stopped to tuck the uneven edges into her skirt. She had washed her face but made do with running careless fingers through her luxurious hair so that it now tumbled untidily about her face and shoulders.

If he refrained from any open comment, she could see his eyes taking it all in. 'I told you I have to be out early.'

'Oh, all right!' How could she tell him she had scarcely slept because of his stepmother's insinuations? She made a swift dive towards an overall, in an effort to hide the tattered state of her clothes, but his hand stopped her.

'Have you no idea how a good housekeeper should conduct herself? You don't even know how to say good morning to your employer properly!' His hands slid to her shoulders with uncompromising firmness as he looked down on her.

She was reminded suddenly of men she would rather forget, although why Neil Cameron should fit this category when she loved him, she had no idea. 'Take your hands off me!' she cried, before she could stop herself. 'I detest them!'

As she shrank back, his mouth tightened, whereas before it had been half smiling. 'Don't I have the right?' he taunted, and far from releasing her, his grip hardened.

'Not—not this sort.'

'Perhaps you could explain?'

Did his voice have to be so silky? She felt herself shiver as the tenseness of his fingers ran through her. 'No,' she swallowed, 'I couldn't. I just dislike having you so near me!'

'You didn't think that last week in the mountains,' he replied grimly. 'And if you say much more I'll show you just how far my rights could go—and there's not a damn thing you could do about it!'

'You wouldn't dare!'

As if again she had tried him too far he pulled her closer, jerking her head back, ruthlessly plundering her protesting lips with his own. He held her thus, cruelly careless against him, and the tight little fists she hit him with might have been drops of beneficial rain for all the notice he took.

'Let me go, you beast!'

'You only incite a man with kind words like that,' he mocked as momentarily he allowed her mouth to escape.

Petra lifted a slim leg to kick him and he trapped it neatly with a much stronger, well muscled one of his own, holding her still until the very kitchen began to whirl.

Still she couldn't give in and made a wild swipe at him with her one free hand. 'It's only because you think you're stronger!' she panted irrationally.

'What should I do to prove it?' he growled, deep in his throat, his eyes sweeping over her dishevelled shirt which was showing some inches of bared skin. 'Come here, my little rebel, my cousin of centuries ago!'

His mouth caught hers again as he lowered his head and when somehow she managed to resist him he slipped an experienced hand beneath her shirt. After this her defences crumbled under the arousing magic of his touch, and he held her firmly until the last of her rebellious tremors were subdued.

When his lips left her now completely responsive mouth she made no attempt to move other than to encircle his strong neck plaintively with drowsy, unsatisfied fingers.

'If it was autumn and everyone gone,' he murmured threateningly, 'I would simply carry you upstairs.'

Perhaps because this related so closely to Fay Cameron's suspicions, Petra felt herself growing cold. It was like a pool of iced water on a hot day, irresistible, but shocking on impact. But before she could accuse him he had moved, so swiftly that she blinked he left her, and she was left with the uneasy feeling that he had spoken deliberately to shock her to her senses.

He was holding his coffee cup again and as she stared at him, bemused, she couldn't see one tremor anywhere.

His eyes were faintly amused, she didn't see they were also watchful, so his next words jolted her, nearly as much as his previous ones had done. 'Now perhaps you might tell me why you're in such a filthy mood this morning? Fay was in your room last night. Has this anything to do with it?'

'No ...' Startled, Petra stared at him. How had he known?

'You could try confiding in me. Once you got the habit it shouldn't be as overpoweringly difficult as it seems now.'

Petra flinched, his sarcasm not going unnoticed. But there were some things a girl had to work out for herself, and she wasn't going to involve Mrs Cameron unnecessarily. Mrs Cameron could have been acting out of the goodness of her heart. Anyway, it might not be wise to tell Neil anything. He could turn out to dislike gossip as much as the next man, and it was no use putting words into the enemy's mouth.

Why she should be suddenly thinking of him as an enemy she didn't know. 'Mrs Cameron just looked in to see if I was comfortable,' she supplied vaguely, looking down at her toes.

'Ah, I see.' His voice was smooth. There was nothing by which Petra could judge whether he believed her or not. 'Well,' he put down his coffee cup with a decisive ring, just as she was thinking of bestirring herself about his meal. 'I'll be back about nine, baby. Be sure you're ready. I'm also taking Janey.'

'What about your breakfast?' she stammered, nearly feeling ashamed of herself.

His eyes mocked her from the doorway. 'I can't say I'm completely satisfied, honey, but I'll make do with what I've had until—later.'

Never in a thousand years could Petra have described the trip to Calgary as entirely successful, but it did have much to recommend it. Neil not only took Janey but David as well, and David, if no one else, was delighted with his excursion. Never having flown on a private plane before, he

made no attempt to hide his excitement, although careful
to do everything Neil told him. As his comments grew
boyishly wilder even Janey was affected by his enthusiasm
and fell to teasing him happily until both she and David
collapsed in a series of stifled giggles.

Petra found herself glancing at Janey with some surprise, feeling oddly warmed towards the girl. Perhaps Janey
wasn't so bad after all. Away from her mother she often
seemed an entirely different person. Frowning, Petra
looked down at her fingers, wondering uneasily if she was
being completely fair. While Mrs Cameron might not
seem a very heart-warming kind of person, she had been
widowed since Janey was an infant. Even though she was
comfortably off it must have been a lonely business bringing up a young child on her own. Perhaps she needed
sympathy rather than criticism, even if she wasn't always
easy to get on with.

Still frowning, Petra raised her eyes to stare out through
the window. There was so much space and tranquillity here
that everything should surely be peaceful. Yet there were
undercurrents at the ranch, the same as anywhere else. As
if their earlier encounter hadn't been enough, she had had
another skirmish in the office with Neil before they had
left. When he had summoned her she had intended to make
the most of such an opportunity by having a lot of things
sorted out, but he had made it so brief that she seemed
scarcely to have got further than the door before he was
pushing her out again.

To begin with she had told him she wasn't going to
Calgary or anywhere else. This firm declaration he had
tossed aside impatiently, without so much as bothering to
reply. Then he had given her a large roll of notes, and
when she had asked with amazement what she was supposed to do with so much money, he had answered that
it would buy her clothes.

'I haven't gone closely into your financial circumstances,
Petronella. I'm merely concluding, recalling our last little
argument here, that you haven't any. You've been working for over a week, so you can take this as wages—some

in advance, if you like. I refuse to have a scarecrow as my housekeeper, so you can take it or leave it.'

Her eyes speaking volumes, Petra had been consumed by a proud inclination to leave it, or throw it in the garbage bin, but something about the taut shape of his mouth had warned her she was skating on very thin ice. That such wonderfully satisfying gestures were luxuries she must deny herself. Blinking, she had glanced at him, her anger turning to uncertainty. It was no use crying for the moon when she must work for David's schooling, and maybe, so far as her clothes went, Neil had a point. She was indeed beginning to look as he indelicately hinted, and she knew a sudden irresistible longing to have some nicer things than she was wearing. 'Thank you,' she had said, at last, wondering despairingly just how much more she was going to have to thank him for in the years to come.

'You're welcome!' he had retorted dryly, and no more had been said about her not going to Calgary.

David, having apparently tired of spotting landmarks en route, had transferred his enthusiastic attention to the plane's controls, and Neil was explaining briefly how the whole system worked. He also, as David's interest continued, told him a little of how the Air Transport of Canada was run. Of how Canadian airways scheduled flights were made every day to almost every country in the world, Air Canada being the principal carrier. He added that Pacific Western, owned by Alberta, flew many thousands of people every year. Petra noticed, with an odd little ache in her heart, how David listened eagerly to every word, and it was very plain to see that his admiration for Neil was growing by the minute.

At Calgary Neil announced that he and David would have a look around on their own while Petra and Janey shopped.

Somewhat relieved that she wasn't to suffer the ordeal of having him stand over her, censuring everything she tried on, Petra followed Janey down the crowded sidewalks to the main shopping centre.

Janey halted beside a large departmental store which

looked alike, yet dissimilar to the ones Petra knew at home. While she was still trying to assess the difference, Janey informed her, 'We usually shop here when we aren't in Toronto. Shall we go in or do you want a further look around?'

Petra shook her head while they stepped into an elevator that whirled them silently up to their requested floor. Here, among a breathaking display of fashions, she chose carefully, trying to be thrifty as David was going to need a lot of school things. Janey, on the other hand, spent much more extravagantly, putting everything down on account. This, she assured Petra blithely, Neil would settle.

'Especially when he knows I'm collecting for my trousseau,' she laughed gaily.

Petra glanced at her doubtfully, hoping she wasn't being too optimistic. No engagement had yet been announced. 'Does this mean it's all settled?' she asked tentatively.

'Not exactly,' Janey still smiled, 'but it's always been understood that one day Oliver and I will marry. It's simply a matter of getting round to settling a date. Last night he said we'd have to get thinking of it seriously, one of these days.'

Which didn't sound like a man head over heels in love, although it did sound as if he really felt, in some way, committed. Perhaps, as Neil suggested, he just needed a little push. Janey certainly didn't seem suspicious that Oliver's reticence was because of Petra, although her eyes were occasionally wary when she glanced at her. 'Perhaps Oliver will ask you the next time he comes over,' Petra said lightly.

Janey, to her surprise, immediately agreed. 'He's coming tomorrow and will probably stay over, so if there's not too many people around, he might.'

Was that just a casual remark or was it a pointed hint? Petra wondered wryly, as she helped Janey choose several more things before making a final decision about her own. She might be wise to make herself scarce tomorrow evening; at least it could do no harm. Quickly she purchased three sober dresses, one for evening wear, the other two for about the kitchen, with an eye to her position. Unable to resist it at the last moment, she added a long flowery one which wasn't practical for anything but looking decorative in, and after paying for it she stuffed it quickly out of sight before she could change her mind.

By the time they met Neil and David for a late lunch both girls were exhausted, or almost.

'Neil has promised to take me to the Calgary Stampede,' David smiled at Petra happily. 'It's a proper rodeo and all the ranch-hands will be going. One day I might even take part myself.'

'How nice,' Petra murmured weakly, scarcely able to connect the robust, eager boy in front of her with the pale, thin-shouldered one of a few weeks ago.

Neil ushered them all into the restaurant after a quick drink. David had something long and cool, a huge glass of it which he couldn't finish, so carried it with him to their table. Neil seated himself beside Petra, leaving the opposite seats for the other two. Petra couldn't make up her mind whether it was better to have Neil sitting by her or facing her. This way, at least, he couldn't read her mind!

David chose a salad and the girls followed, while Neil had a steak. The size of the steak, when it arrived, must have been about sixteen ounces, but Canadians, Petra had discovered, ate more than most Europeans, and the portions of meat served in restaurants were very generous compared with British standards. Even on the ranch Petra found she couldn't often manage a sweet after the soup and meat course.

The restaurant Neil had brought them to was very pleasant, with cubicle-like tables. It was only as the meal progressed that she realised it was a little cramped and that most of the time she was too close to him. Her pulse jumped whenever she moved a restless limb and came up against him, and she was continually aware of his gaze on her pale profile each time she turned her head. Yet she couldn't say his attention was entirely unflattering. For the most part he left Janey to entertain David and concentrated on Petra himself.

'Did you have a good morning?' He refilled her glass with a cool, sparkling wine.

'Yes, I suppose so.' She could have told him she was truly pleased with her purchases, but she still felt an odd shame at having to accept his money. Everything seemed rapidly to be becoming more difficult than she had ever imagined.

Wearily she picked up her glass, then found her left hand trapped under his. When she glanced at him blankly, he merely stared back at her and, leaning nearer, asked carefully if she had everything she wanted. His attitude was so like that of an intimate companion that after her pulse steadied she felt a wave of antagonism.

'Please,' she protested, trying to speak lightly under the cover of David's busy chatter, 'what is this?'

For an instant his fingers tightened painfully. 'I thought we were out to convince Oliver you really fancied me?'

'Fancied you!'

'That's what I said.' His fingers found her hurrying pulse and lingered.

'Oh, I see,' she answered, relief paling her cheeks. 'But Oliver isn't here.'

'Janey will tell him. She never misses out on a thing.'

'If Janey thinks he's the least bit interested in me she'll no doubt tell him I made eyes at every man I passed. You could be surplus.'

'To immediate requirements? You could have a point there,' he drawled, 'but we could always make sure. Oliver has always shown considerable respect for my property.'

'I see,' she said again, this time more resignedly, feeling a sudden coolness creeping in at his careless words.

'You'd better begin smiling if I promise to let go of your hand,' he warned, his mouth quirking at the corners, as if to show her exactly how it was done. 'If I have to think of everything myself you'd never know how far I might feel forced to go.'

In spite of an inner reluctance, she found herself obeying wryly. 'As we're in a respectable restaurant I think the most you can do is threaten!'

'But you might not be wise to believe I'm only teasing!'

'Deliberately provoking could be nearer the mark!'

'Perhaps with noble justification,' his voice came dry with a hint of self-mockery. 'If I don't do something to lighten the situation between us it could get out of hand.'

'You couldn't deal with it if it did?' She had no clear idea what he was talking about, but something smouldering at the back of his dark eyes disturbed her unduly.

'You're not ready yet—old enough, if you like, to face up to the consequences of all your highly improbable actions over the past weeks. It behoves a man in my position to keep a cool hand on the controls.'

'Old enough for what?' Her mind fixed on that one point with apprehensive swiftness.

'Honey,' his eyes remained on her clouded, uncertain face, 'I'm years ahead, well past thirty. By comparison you're still an infant.'

It seemed imperative, suddenly, that she should refute this. 'I've grown up!' she said crossly.

'Then you've got to grow some more, and quickly. I will give you, however, another few weeks.'

'How generous!' Where did Oliver come in all this? If only she could gauge the exact content of what he said! Yet she couldn't bring herself to ask him to explain, some part of her shying away from a final showdown. Instead, she attacked him nervously, her agitation clearly demonstrated by her quickening breath. 'I sensed you would be devious, the first time I saw you. Just like my Cameron in the painting!' Even after speaking them, she didn't realise her significant choice of words.

'What are you two on about?' Janey interrupted curiously, as David turned his attention elsewhere.

'Our ancestor,' Neil enlightened his stepsister with an unusual quirk of triumph. 'Petronella was making some interesting remarks.'

'Why do you call her Petronella?' Janey exclaimed, looking from one to the other. 'She always insists that the rest of us call her Petra.'

Neil returned her expectant glance suavely. 'I like her

full name, especially when I'm the only one allowed to use it.'

'Why——' At loss for words, Petra's indignant eyes widened on his, not perceiving that the gaze she turned on him gave Janey food for thought.

The girl giggled, 'I hope Petra knows what sort of man you are!'

'She's getting the general idea.'

Janey grinned mischievously at a confused Petra. 'Almost every woman in the territory is out to get him. Can you wonder he's spoilt? Don't let him charm you.'

'Your advice,' Neil replied soberly, 'could be too late.'

Petra tried to break in, only to be forestalled by an enthusiastic Janey. 'I know just how you feel, Petra! I'm exactly the same way about Oliver, so I don't mind Neil being so outspoken. It sort of clears the air.'

Suddenly remembering where it was, Petra jerked her trembling hand from under Neil's lean fingers. It was all part of the act, she understood, but Neil's light banter hurt horribly. She felt irrationally glad when David joined in the conversation, but she had also a sick impression that she was alone in a rudderless boat in stormy seas, and could only go where the tide swept her.

CHAPTER TEN

PETRA knew Oliver was coming to dinner and staying overnight. Oliver didn't play all the time, apparently, the main reason for this visit being to enable him to buy some pedigree Herefords which Neil sold annually from his herds. This, Janey had confided, usually put Oliver in a responsible frame of mind and Petra suspected she had set her heart on inveigling a definite proposal. She didn't say so outright as she always pretended to take Oliver completely for granted, but today Petra had sensed her hidden anxiety and secret determination.

Privately Petra vowed she would do everything she could to help things along. It wasn't as if Oliver didn't intend marrying Janey. One could really see it a mile off! If she hadn't been convinced he really did love Janey she would have left it severely alone, in spite of Neil's threats. It simply seemed to her that two very nice young people could be extremely happy, given a little encouragement. All they were doing at the moment was wasting time.

She prepared the evening meal, leaving it cooking in charge of Mrs Edwards while she ran upstairs. Janey had been closeted in her room half the afternoon and after a quick shower Petra dragged on her dressing gown and went to seek her out. A quick tap on Janey's door admitted her.

'Oh, it's you!' Already dressed in soft silk, Janey glanced at Petra impatiently before returning to contemplate her unruly hair in the mirror. 'Just look at this! Away from the city I can never do a thing with it, and the condition of my hair means the difference between being plain or pretty! It's not naturally gorgeous all the time like yours. It needs professional attention.'

'Here, let me help.' Forgetting her excuse for invading Janey's bedroom, as she wasn't apparently going to need it,

Petra reached for a brush from the selection of expensive ones on the toilet-table. Within minutes she had transformed Janey's hair by brushing the lacquer-soaked, pretentious style into something much more simple. 'You don't suit it all screwed up on top of your head,' she smiled. 'Take a good look if you don't believe me.'

Janey did, her eyes rounding with astonishment as she stared in her long mirror. 'Gee!' she exclaimed impulsively, 'you're a wizard. Where did you learn?'

'I didn't,' Petra laughed. 'I never bother with my own, although,' she added teasingly, 'I can see I have potential. One day I might train as a hairdresser.'

Janey was still admiring her new self and she took Petra's lighthearted comment seriously. 'I'm sure our hairdresser in Toronto would take you on. You are good—I look quite different. Oliver's sure to be knocked out! I think I'll go and show Mother first, though. She has the same problem as I have in the country.'

Picking up a pair of discarded jeans from the floor, Petra laid them neatly over a chair before turning to study Janey again.

Janey continued, as she searched untidily for a handkerchief, 'I hope Neil's in a good mood tonight. He's been very unpredictable since we went to Calgary the other day. Like a bear with a sore head! Haven't you been treating him properly?'

'I—treating him properly? How do you mean?' Petra, trying to decide how she could advise Janey to use less make-up on her perfectly good skin, spoke abstractedly.

'Well, you know, honey. Blowing hot and cold.'

'Not really.' Petra swallowed, recalling uneasily how, on the trip to Calgary, her better relationship with Neil had seemed suddenly to deteriorate after lunch into a series of terse arguments. He had insisted, when he'd got down to itemising what she had purchased, that she hadn't bought enough. He had also insisted, when she had pointed out she had left money for David's school clothes, that he would buy everything David needed himself. None of which had notably lightened the atmosphere!

'Come to think of it, Petra, you've been rather pale yourself since then.' Janey scrutinised Petra's face, her eyes suddenly crafty keen. 'How long have you been here, honey?'

'Several weeks ...'

'You're not—not in any trouble?'

'Trouble?'

'Well,' Janey's laughter tinkled spitefully, 'there's only one sort of trouble a girl gets into with a man.'

'Janey!' Shocked, Petra couldn't bring herself to put it into words. 'You can't possibly mean ...'

'Oh, stay calm, Petra! It happens all the time, all over the world, and Neil's no saint. With a girl like you ...'

'Yes,' Petra prompted, her voice frozen as Janey hesitated, 'a girl like me?'

'I just meant, Petra, you have such an innocent look about you. Oliver says you're a challenge to any man.'

'Thank you,' Petra replied tonelessly, 'but I can assure you your brother and I haven't indulged in—in that kind of thing.'

'Then there's no harm done.' Janey's giggle seemed a trifle forced this time. 'And you know Neil's just my step-brother and normally I see very little of him. For pity's sake don't repeat what I've said. He might not like it.'

Petra sighed. While she knew such matters as Janey referred to weren't sacrosanct any more, she had never got used to discussing them casually. During the year she had worked she had learnt that sex was a fairly commonplace topic of conversation, but she still wasn't sure it should be bandied about as it was.

Janey, as if her nerve had for once deserted her, ran off without waiting to exchange another word, leaving Petra to close the door before going back to her own room.

Scarcely knowing what she was doing, Petra began to dress. More and more she was beginning to realise just how impossible was her situation. It might be all right just now, with Janey and her mother here, but what would happen after they had gone? It was obvious that Mrs Cameron was already speculating, and sharing her suspicions with her daughter. How many others would, before long, be the recipients of her doubtful confidences? Janey might, of course, have been making it up. She wasn't exactly an endearing kind of person. She didn't believe in sheathing her claws when she felt like getting at someone. Unhappily Petra trailed over to where her painting of the Scottish Cameron, once more restored to his previous position on her wall, regarded her with his usual enigmatic expression. 'If only I didn't love him so much,' she whispered aloud, thinking of Neil.

All through dinner Petra was quiet. She had put on her new long dress, the dark-hued one, and tied her long pale hair back with a confining ribbon. She had left off every scrap of make-up apart from a few strokes of lipstick, but if she had hoped to look uninterestingly plain she was mistaken. The rather severe hairstyle suited her, throwing her excellent bone structure into relief and making her appear quite extraordinarily beautiful. Oliver kept glancing at her, as if puzzled, and the situation was only saved by Petra's lack of vitality. While Janey chattered, with increasing excitement, Petra sat pale and strained, toying with her food, barely able to glance at anybody. Consequently Oliver's wandering attention was drawn back to Janey, and he shrugged, as if deciding, once and for all, that her bright gaiety was preferable to the young cousin's moodiness.

After dinner, as usual, David went to bed, and after bringing in the coffee Petra intended retiring too, but to her dismay Oliver asked her to play.

'Either the piano or your guitar,' he requested. 'Perhaps Janey might like to hear you sing. It could be most romantic.'

Petra, pleading tiredness, refused, annoyed that he had mentioned it as neither of the other two women knew anything about these last two accomplishments and she had no wish to increase their guarded antagonism further by stealing any of the limelight when Oliver was around.

'I'm going to take Neil's coffee out to the porch,' she said quickly. 'I promised him.'

She couldn't recall that she had, but regardless of

whether they believed her or not she made her escape and found Neil sitting where she had hoped he would be.

'I've brought you coffee,' she explained, as a light query leapt to his eyes at the sight of her. 'I didn't think you would want to miss it while it's still hot.' The excuse seemed feeble and she wished she might have avoided him by going straight upstairs instead of following the first notion to come into her head. She put his cup down quickly by his side and made to turn away from his calculating glance, but he grasped her arm.

'You've been looking pale all evening,' he said grimly. 'Has someone been getting at you?'

'No,' she replied over quickly, but although his eyes narrowed he didn't pursue the matter—not immediately.

'Come and sit by me.' Catching her off balance, he gave her arm a slight tug, bringing her down beside him. 'This is all getting a bit much, isn't it?'

Because he sounded so surprisingly gentle and it seemed a long time since anyone had been gentle with her, Petra collapsed unresisting, like a highly strung, delicate flower at his feet, her cheek hidden in a kind of abject surrender against his knee.

'Hi, what is this?' His voice, as near startled as she had ever heard it, hardened perceptibly. 'You're sure no one's upset you?'

If only she could tell him! As she rested blindly against him, seeking only a fleeting comfort, she came near to breaking point. The moment passed as she gained a precarious control and she shook her head as he asked again. Rashly she heard herself saying instead, 'You've been ignoring me since Calgary.'

'Yes.' He offered no excuse, or explanation, and her head bent further.

'Has it to do with me?'

'You could say.' The hand on her shoulder moved slowly.

Petra's heart sank. Maybe Neil, too, had heard rumours? She felt the sting of sharp tears in her eyes. 'I don't mean to annoy you.'

'Annoy me?' He paused enigmatically, running his fingers gently over her soft hair, pressing her face to his thigh as she made to move away from him. She heard his slightly frustrated sigh. 'You don't annoy me, but you must know you affect me. I'm only human, Petronella, and you're a very attractive girl. Sometimes I'm ready to admit I want you, but wanting and possessing are two different things.'

'Have they to be?' Quietly relaxing, as his caressing hand slowly eased the hard tension from her slender shoulders, she could think of nothing she wanted more than to belong to him.

He gave a taut laugh. 'Speaking generally, I take it?'

'No,' she sighed, the darkness of the past hours giving way to a tremulous yearning. 'Well, what's the difference?'

'Every difference, my dear child. I want my brains examined, for instance, for ever allowing the past few weeks to happen. I'm trying to wade my way sensibly through a vast muddle and won't allow any more complications. Not yet!'

Unconsciously Petra trailed a slender white arm over his knees. 'How could I become a complication?'

'Easily.' In no way did he spare her. 'You're young and very desirable and I'm not a particularly unselfish male.'

So, in some of the things she'd said, hadn't Janey been right? All men were the same, even Neil Cameron! Her heart ached, but there was no desire within her to evade him as there had been with other men. She accepted Neil's dominance with only a slight quiver of regret, a regret which might swiftly disappear before another, more consuming emotion.

'I thought you were different,' she sighed, because this seemed the more sensible thing to say.

He didn't pretend to misunderstand. 'Don't rely on it, Petronella. There are those of us who are perhaps a shade better in some respects, a few degrees more refined. But given certain situations there might be little to choose among any of us.'

'I don't know how I would feel about you.' Such a confession seemed to cost her a great deal, but it seemed she had to make it. 'If I were to belong to you.'

She heard his breathing deepen a little without being really aware of it. 'There's only one way to answer that, Petronella, and words don't come into it. There are, however, things we must discuss before we reach other stages. But not tonight.'

There was suddenly Janey's light laughter mingling with Oliver's as they swept from the living room, past the couple on the porch. Startled, Petra glanced up, watching them disappear. 'Do you think they saw us?' she whispered, conscious how she sat on the floor.

'I should think it very likely,' Neil drawled, his eyes flickering over the alluring picture she made against his knee.

'What will they think?' Covered in confusion, she made to draw away, but he held her still.

'Don't worry your head about them any more,' he said cryptically. 'As far as they're concerned I'm hoping our worries will soon be over.

'You're sure?'

'I could be a mind-reader,' he teased.

Her eyes were heavy as she tried to study the face above her. 'How?'

'Come on.' Gently he released her, ignoring her query as he pulled her firmly to her feet. 'You're tired. I think, bed.'

'Can't I stay here with you?' She didn't know quite how dazed she looked, what her face unconsciously betrayed.

'No!' he was emphatic. 'Come on, I'll even take you upstairs.'

Quietly submissive, she obeyed, as if without a will of her own, but as she got to her feet she swayed and he caught her, lifting her to him.

'I'll carry you.'

'Yes.' Suddenly she was so tired she couldn't fight any more. She was glad to rely on him. Closing her weighted lids, she simply put her arms around his neck and nestled closer against his broad shoulder. She didn't see Mrs

Cameron coming into the wide hall, nor did she realise that Neil did but gave no indication.

'Neil ...' At her bedroom door Petra pulled herself together wearily, 'I haven't seen Mrs Edwards. The coffee things!'

'Leave them to me.'

The door was thrust open and he carried her over the threshold like something very precious.

'Neil ...?'

'Leave it for now,' he warned, and dropped a sudden urgent kiss on her warm, half parted mouth before quietly closing the door behind him.

Petra learnt that Oliver and Janey were engaged next morning at breakfast. 'If you hadn't been in such a hurry to get to bed last night we would have told you then,' Janey smiled archly.

Trying to be generous, Petra offered her congratulations and asked if the wedding was to be soon.

'About two months,' Janey giggled, restored to humour. 'That will give me time to get my trousseau together. You might even agree to being my maid of honour. A little Scottish cousin should be quite a novelty!'

Petra refrained from saying that she was probably no more Scottish than Janey now, and she privately wondered how Janey could bear to wait two whole months. Wistfully she considered how she might have felt if she had been engaged to Neil.

Neil, when she spoke to him about it, said very little. 'Janey wants to get married in Toronto. I suppose it's to be expected as she's spent most of her life there. Oliver's parents are divorced, but his mother remarried and lives there too, so it appears to suit everyone.'

Petra, who had thought Janey would want to be married from the ranch, said abstractedly, 'And it's not for two months!'

'You don't sound approving.'

She flushed at the dryness of his tones, her momentary

confusion prompting an unguarded reply. 'It must seem a lifetime if one's in love.'

'But you're not in love, are you, Petronella?' he challenged callously. 'You can't talk with any authority.'

She said nothing, lowering her revealing eyes from his unnerving scrutiny.

'You could have been in love, of course.' His voice was suddenly grim. 'A girl like you couldn't be without some experience.'

Painfully, Petra's gaze clashed with his. So his thoughts ran along much the same lines as his stepmother's! Her face whitened visibly. 'Everyone is entitled to his own opinion, but it could be fair to ensure that it's correct.'

'Yes,' he agreed moodily, staring at her, as if he might devour her with his eyes, 'there are several things I've to set right about you, Petronella. All in good time. This you need more than me.'

Bewildered, Petra stared at him, trying to make sense of his enigmatical statements. 'Don't you believe a girl of my age capable of knowing her own mind?'

'Most of the time,' he conceded briefly. 'But there are some decisions that need absolute adult concentration.'

'You still think of me as a child?'

'If we must go over all that again, yes! In some ways you couldn't be otherwise.'

'But not completely?'

'No,' his eyes wandered with reluctant grimness to her trembling mouth, 'not by a long way, but I must leave you some form of self-protection.'

'What if I don't need it, want it?'

He considered her touching bravado derisively. 'Like most females you have your own means of ensnaring a man, but let me tell you, my little witch, it doesn't entirely work with me. Not yet, anyhow.'

'Because you won't let it—you despise the lot of us!' She was wound up, tense with the force of unfamiliar, devastating feelings which had nothing to do with the calm warmth of the morning. 'You . . .'

'Be quiet!' He was suddenly curt and, as she made to speak again, he hauled her impatiently to him, bending his dark head as he ruthlessly crushed her lips beneath his. He did it as if he couldn't help himself and didn't much care if he hurt her or not. Eventually, just as everything began to whirl, he released her. 'I'd like to go on doing just that until you couldn't think any more, Petronella. Until a lot of the nonsense you've gathered about me is relegated to where it belongs—the scrapheap! You jump to too many unflattering conclusions, all of which need sorting out.'

Dazed, she stepped away from him, seeking the saneness of a little distance. Her heart was beating so loudly she was sure he must hear it if she stayed close, and there was a need to control a driving impulse to confess how much she loved him, despite everything. But staring up into his hard, good-looking face, she found she could say nothing.

'Janey,' Neil continued absently, his eyes on Petra's flushed cheeks, 'is going to stay with Oliver and his father for a few days, then she's going with Fay back to Toronto. You might run along and help to get her organised. She's the most scatterbrained girl on God's earth and I wouldn't want anything to happen to change her mind, not at this stage.'

The kitchen seemed oddly empty after he had gone and Petra began automatically to pack the dishwasher. She could have told Neil, if he had waited, that she had listened to Janey's plans for over an hour at breakfast and that Janey appeared to have competently covered the following weeks, and that not even Oliver might be allowed to interfere with them now. Janey could organise as well as anybody when she had her own interests at heart.

To Petra's surprise Janey wanted to take David with her on her visit to her future father-in-law's ranch, and Neil advised her to let him go.

'Another three weeks and he will be away to school. A short break beforehand could be a help for both of you. How long is it since you've been away from each other for any length of time?'

'Not since—not since Father died ...'

'Then I would say you need this. David won't feel the break half as much if he has this small one first.'

Petra wasn't sure why she should feel so apprehensive, especially when she had grown quite used to the idea of David being away at school. Perhaps, as Neil pointed out, a short separation, not so far away, might benefit them both. If she first made certain he would be well cared for?

'What's Oliver's ranch like?' She looked at Neil with such obvious uncertainty that no one could mistake her silent plea for reassurance.

Realising this, and without any hesitation, which might have furthered her doubts, he replied, 'Big and very, very nice. Much more of a show place than this. He'll enjoy himself, you can take my word for it. Janey's responsible, she's twenty-six, and she's going to love showing him around.'

'Yes ...' Petra knew Janey and David had grown friendly and that Janey was good with the boy. It was just that she felt so anxious about him. It was terribly important that no harm befell him. 'Is Mrs Cameron going too?' The thought had only just occurred to her.

'No, she'll stay here and accompany Janey to Toronto next week, as I've already told you. Joe Hurd, Oliver's father, and Fay don't hit it off, although he likes Janey.'

Suddenly deciding no useful purpose could be served by standing in David's way, not when he was so keen to go, Petra capitulated. 'I'm sorry if I haven't seemed too keen,' she tried to explain. 'I have to look after him, you see. I find myself getting more and more anxious that something might happen.'

'You can't take over the role of a parent, Petronella, not completely. I shouldn't advise you to keep on trying. You'll only wear yourself out and that would be of no help to anyone. I'd revert to the status of sister, if I were you, and let your future husband take most of the responsibility.'

'But I haven't got one.'

'No,' he smiled condescendingly, 'you haven't, at that, but you could have.'

How could she argue with this without betraying to Neil that he was the only one she wanted, so consequently that particular comment was a waste of time! She tried to smile back at him lightly, but failed.

'In the meantime,' Neil suggested smoothly, 'how about letting me step in? I'll go with them this afternoon and see for myself how David's likely to settle. If he doesn't take to it I promise to bring him home.'

How nice it would be if they could call the ranch home always! Petra taunted herself inwardly over such an impossible wish. 'I wouldn't want you to make such a journey because of me,' she protested. 'I know how busy you are. Jake said . . .'

'Never mind about Jake,' Neil retorted firmly. 'Joe Hurd has been buying a stock bull from a cousin at an extremely good price, but isn't sure now that he has a bargain. He wants my advice. I shall probably stay and return in the morning.'

They all went down to the sheds to see them off. Even Mrs Cameron came and, as she rarely strayed more than five yards from the ranch house, this seemed further evidence that she was extremely pleased about Janey's engagement. After David had said his farewells, Neil instructed Jake to get him settled in the helicopter, then, in full view of everyone, kissed Petra goodbye.

'Just in case some predatory male is looking,' he teased, eyeing her pink face with satisfaction before turning on his heels.

Numbly she stared after his tall figure. He hadn't waited for any reply and she thought she knew why. He wanted Oliver to believe she was no longer hankering after him. Bleakly she tried to raise a smile in response to David's enthusiastic waving, the hurt in her heart not subsiding. Not even David appeared to have any real regrets about leaving her!

After they had gone Mrs Cameron walked back to the

house with her, but unfortunately her happier mood seemed to have faded, for she scarcely spoke to Petra at all. Petra found herself glancing towards the woman anxiously, wondering how she might explain Neil's kiss. She must tell Mrs Cameron it was nothing to worry about. That he had merely been attempting to ensure Janey's happiness in a roundabout fashion. Then, deciding it would be almost impossible to put into words, Petra said nothing. After all, time would prove the emptiness of Neil's gesture better than anything she might say now.

It was quiet without Neil and David. Feeling suddenly weary as well as heartsore, Petra could scarcely find the energy to change for dinner. Irrationally, when there was no one specially to see her, she put on her new flowered dress and made up carefully. At least it might prove to Fay that Petra didn't just dress to please her stepson!

To say dinner was a strain would have been putting it mildly, the atmosphere being so thick with undercurrents Petra felt she could have cut it with a knife. But it wasn't until after coffee that Mrs Cameron attacked, to begin with only with words.

'How much longer,' she asked, staring at Petra coldly, 'are you going to stay here?'

Decidedly shaken by such alien tones, Petra stared at her. 'I thought we'd discussed all—that?'

'That's no answer!' Fay retorted icily.

Petra decided nervously it would be better not to provoke Mrs Cameron further, if she could help it. She had a taut look about her, almost as if she wanted to strike, and not just verbally. 'I'm not sure I can give you one,' she said carefully. 'Hadn't you better ask Neil?'

'Why should I?' Fay's voice rose spitefully. 'I saw today, quite clearly with my own eyes, exactly why he lets you stay here!'

So that was it. She had been right all along. Mrs Cameron had been incensed by seeing her in Neil's close embrace. Well, maybe she wasn't altogether to be blamed, but still Petra couldn't bring herself to say she would be gone at the first opportunity. Because Mrs Cameron somehow set her teeth on edge with her half-hidden innuendoes, she heard herself say flatly, 'It wasn't what you think.'

'There's some simple explanation?'

Petra tried to ignore the heavy sarcasm on Mrs Cameron's tongue. Better to remain calm. 'I'm sorry,' she whispered, 'I don't think ...'

'You're sorry!' Mrs Cameron's rage mounted. 'If only that were true!'

'True?' Desperately Petra tried to control her faltering voice, her shaking limbs. 'Probably it's not,' she admitted daringly, rashly giving way to a momentary defiance. 'I don't think I've anything to be really sorry for, not so far as you're concerned. I hate to seem rude but I don't think either David or I have done you any harm.'

Mrs Cameron was clearly incensed. Normally the possessor of a quick temper, something about Petra's white, stricken face, combined with the amazingly courageous angle of her softly rounded chin, aroused her furiously. 'Don't you know,' she cried, her eyes flashing, 'that anything which concerns Neil concerns me as well!'

'I didn't realise,' Petra muttered weakly, her nerve failing her again.

Before such abject defeat Mrs Cameron's raging confidence surged. 'How do we know you're anything but a common little adventuress? You come here, disrupt all our lives, what are we to think! Neil is in love with a very nice girl in Toronto. How do you imagine she's going to feel when she discovers you're here?'

'A girl in Toronto?' Try as she might, Petra failed to keep the despair from her voice or a sudden startling greyness from her cheeks, 'Do you mean he's going to marry her?'

'What else—when she's so crazy about him?' Fay retorted wildly.

Painfully Petra tried to raise her head. 'I wouldn't do anything to prevent it, if that's what you mean.'

Pressing an undoubted advantage, Fay rasped, 'You have intelligence, you must see your presence here won't help!'

Dully Petra agreed. 'I'll speak to Neil, then I'll leave right away.'

'Don't speak to him,' Fay said sharply, 'just go! You could be gone before he returns.'

'I can't,' Petra's voice was beseeching. 'There's David, you see, and I couldn't leave without thanking Neil for all he's done for us.'

Her fury getting the better of her in the face of Petra's continuing obstinacy, Fay lost control. In a second she was on her feet, raising her heavily ringed hand to strike the girl impulsively across her face.

'Fay!' It was Neil's voice, his exclamation like a whip-crack, quite sufficient to spin Fay terrifyingly in her tracks, 'Just what the hell do you think you're doing!'

Struck, with a frightening apprehension, Fay couldn't reply. She watched speechlessly as her stepson, after slaying her with another glance, strode swiftly to Petra's side and put a protective arm around her. The anger in his eyes as he regarded the growing red marks on Petra's cheek was scaring.

It was Petra who broke the awful silence. She was as stunned as Fay by his unexpected appearance, but there was an urge inside her to soothe him, 'It's nothing Neil, please!' She couldn't bear to look at Mrs Cameron, but she must protect her from the wrath which surged so clearly in Neil's black face. 'I'm quite all right, Neil. Your stepmother might have lost her temper, but not without some justification, I'm afraid.'

'What justification?' Still keeping a tight hold of Petra, he turned with tiger-like swiftness on Fay, whose face visibly paled.

'I—I know you might feel annoyed with me, Neil, but it seems you've got yourself into a situation here which needs sorting out. I was simply trying to do my best for all concerned, as no doubt Petra will vouch. You should appreciate it.'

'Not the way you were doing it!' His glacial glance left her to soften down on the girl who still trembled against him. 'Petronella darling, could you leave us. I'll join you in a few minutes.'

Feeling numb with a shocked unhappiness, Petra obeyed, but instead of staying in the house she ran out of the wide open door and made for the creek. Here, about half a mile away from the homestead, there were stretches of shallow water teeming with wildlife. It had become a favourite spot of hers, a kind of refuge when things got too much for her, and blindly she ran towards it now, uncaring that the tangled undergrowth caught at her flimsy new dress, tearing it outrageously. If Neil really wanted to, after his stepmother had talked to him, he probably knew where to find her as he had come across her here before on more than one occasion.

This evening, however, the still water seemed to offer none of its usual consolation. In the half light Petra stared at it despairingly. Neil might be annoyed with her for running away, but how could she have done otherwise when she had been the cause of so much trouble? None of this was really Mrs Cameron's fault, as he would soon discover. He would soon see, as she did, that all Petra's plans had been preposterous and that Fay had been quite justified in getting alarmed. In Fay's shoes, Petra could not but admit, she might have felt the same way. With a small, tortured moan she flung herself down on the night-chilled grass and began to sob, unhappiness tearing at the aching void that was her heart.

'Petronella!'

Only one person called her that. It must be Neil. Perhaps if she lay still he wouldn't see her and would go away. She hadn't taken into account the gay material of her dress and she heard him crashing through the brushwood towards her, startling some young killdeer birds into a wild clamour nearby.

'Petronella! Come here, darling.' Suddenly, before she could move to escape him, he was kneeling beside her, drawing her resisting body into his arms, soothing her as he would a child. Gently but firmly he turned her to him, smoothing the long, tumbled hair from her hot face, ex-

amining closely now the long scratch left by the impact
of Fay's ring. Through the gathering darkness his eyes still
glittered with anger, 'I'm sorry, child,' his face hardened,
'I would have done anything to prevent this happening,
but I don't think Fay will bother you again.'

'Oh, Neil,' Petra's voice was a small cry of anguish as
she stared up at him, 'don't you think I've done enough
harm without making more trouble between you and your
family?'

'I scarcely regard Fay as family,' he retorted curtly. 'She's
certainly never been any mother to me. But regardless of
that I've always tried to do my best for her, and nothing
could excuse her attacking you as she did today.'

Anxiously Petra tried to pull away from him. 'Please
Neil, don't judge her too harshly. I don't think she ever intended to slap me. You must admit my being here might
cause anyone in her position to wonder. She just lost control. I don't believe she meant any real harm.'

'Whether this is true or not we won't be seeing much of
her for a while,' he rejoined grimly. 'I'm afraid I straightened her out on a few things, something which has been
long overdue. You only brought things to a head. Whether
we have her back at the ranch or not depends very much
on how she conducts herself in the future. Our future—because I love you, my darling.'

Before she could prevent him he had pulled her swiftly
to him again and began kissing her fiercely, his mouth
finding hers with urgent pressure before seeking the soft
curve of her neck and shoulders which her torn dress had
left bare. She felt herself responding with compulsive
passion, in spite of the fright which still lingered in her
body, as his lips returned to hers and his hand on her hip
held her closely against him. She was aware of him and
longed for him with every bit of her and didn't know
where she found the strength to finally push him away.

'Neil, your stepmother said you're in love with a girl in
Toronto. How can you love me?'

Derisively he smiled but made no attempt to reclaim her
immediately, even though his eyes smouldered possessively

over her. 'There are several girls in Toronto and elsewhere that Fay would like to see me married to, but as I care for none of them you can dismiss them from your mind. You're the one I'm going to marry, whether or not you're agreeable,' he added coolly.

Her heart pounding furiously, Petra stared at him while his eyes glittered over her implacably, leaving her in no doubt as to the restraint he was exercising in not dragging her back into his arms. 'You're just making that up!' she cried despairingly. 'Oh, Neil, why torture me so?'

He made a rough gesture towards her, then stopped himself, as if acknowledging that there were things to put right between them. 'The first time I saw you, Petronella, I told Jake you were the girl I was going to marry. If you don't believe me then you must go and ask him. Why do you imagine I let you talk me into allowing you to stay as long as you did? To begin with I was maybe only trying to prove I didn't really want you, but I merely became more convinced I couldn't let you go.'

'Yet you wanted me to leave with you when you went to Toronto?'

'Yes,' his mouth went grim, 'but only because I planned to follow you back to London, to propose to you in your own home. You see, I didn't realise then that you hadn't any. You were so young, I hoped this would give you time, an opportunity of seeing me in your own familiar surroundings, before making up your mind. I wanted to marry you there, to bring you back here as my bride. When you refused to even come as far as Toronto I naturally felt very frustrated, my love! I decided you didn't care for me, that any emotion you felt was only because I resembled the Cameron in the painting, the man you'd become mysteriously attracted to.'

'He ceased to be you a long time ago, Neil. You must know it's true. I'd never confuse the two of you now!'

'You'd better not,' he growled threateningly. 'There are ways I can make you realise I'm the one who's flesh and blood!'

Heat crept beneath her skin, but there still seemed more

she must apologise for. 'When you returned from Toronto, that night in your office, I threatened you with your ancestor's debt. Neil—I'm sorry . . .'

'So you should be, Petronella!' His mouth quirked. 'I could have shown you a letter of acknowledgement, signed by your ancestor in the eighteen-eighties, showing the debt repaid in full.'

Startled beyond words, as the full impact of this information hit her, Petra stammered, 'Why didn't you? I had nowhere to go, you see,' she said brokenly, 'and no money. It was terrible having to threaten you as I did, but I didn't know what else I could do. There was David—but you should have told me about the money being repaid!'

'Yes,' he agreed wryly, frowning at her feverish face, 'perhaps I should. I must confess I didn't for two reasons. Firstly I was stunned, young lady, then so infuriated that I vowed there and then that you must go. Once you were out of sight I was determined I would soon forget you. Yet you'd barely been gone half an hour before I had to come chasing after you, full of every excuse for doing so but the right one!'

Her eyes dilated. 'I thought you merely followed me for fear I might run to Oliver? I never intended doing that.'

'I know, child. It wasn't for Janey's sake that I came. I was simply terrified you were really attracted to him, which is quite a confession! Then up in the mountains I made an amazing discovery. You clung to me, not just for comfort, you really wanted to be in my arms. After that nothing could stop me, but maybe I was too bent on having Janey and every other complication out of the way before getting things properly settled between us. But if I didn't put it into words you must have guessed how I felt each time I kissed you?'

Bewildered, Petra could only shake her head, still scarcely able to take in all he was telling her. 'Why did you return this evening?' she asked tautly, her heart racing. 'How did you know I wanted you?'

'I felt something was wrong. I couldn't settle. Loving you as completely as I do, I know you're already so much a part of me that, instinctively, I seemed to know you needed help.'

Petra shivered, yet she found she couldn't take Fay's behaviour too much to heart. Some time in the future, she felt, somehow she and Fay would be friends. She would do everything she could to make it so.

'Another thing,' Neil was saying, 'David and I have been doing some talking this afternoon. He's told me a lot about your life in London since your father died—the jobs you had, the men you didn't want. He isn't too young to be aware of at least some of the things which drove you to come here. Oh, Petronella,' he exclaimed huskily, 'I could almost beat you for not telling me yourself.'

'I'd rather you kissed me.' She spoke quickly, because she felt she must be shameless, but suddenly she yearned for him. So much.

'I must, because I can't resist you any longer, you little witch.' Passion smouldered in his dark eyes as his arms swiftly drew her unprotesting body to him again and he bent her back to the grass-covered earth. His mouth kissed gently every inch of her face and neck before reaching her trembling lips.

'I love you,' she whispered, against his urgent mouth, unable to help herself.

'Not nearly as much as I love you,' Neil retorted thickly, his hand exploring the curve of her breast which her torn dress had bared, 'but I'll teach you, my darling. You're young enough to learn—to be exactly as I want you. We'll be married right away. Before David goes to school. We have his blessing, and I'm going to look after him as well.'

The privilege of living here for the rest of her life, even the idea of it was almost too much for her. She must prove to Neil in the future how much she loved him. And now! 'Yes,' she breathed deeply shaken. 'All I want is to love you, marry you. I'm yours, to do with as you choose.'

As he pulled her even closer, she returned the increasing pressure of his mouth, the whole of her responding so passionately to his unspoken demands that he could be left in no doubt that her overwhelming need matched his.

'You're mine!' he murmured, before the moon and stars blacked out.

'For always,' Petra promised fervently, wrapping her slender young arms tightly around his neck.

Harlequin Presents...

The beauty of true romance...

The excitement of world travel...

The splendor of first love...

unique love stories for today's woman

Harlequin Presents...
novels of honest,
twentieth-century love,
with characters who
are interesting, vibrant
and alive.

The elegance of love...
The warmth of romance...
The lure of faraway places...

Four new novels, every
month — wherever
paperbacks are sold.

What readers say about Harlequin Romances

"I feel as if I am in a different world every time I read a Harlequin."

A.T.,* Detroit, Michigan

"Harlequins have been my passport to the world. I have been many places without ever leaving my doorstep."

P.Z., Belvedere, Illinois

"I like Harlequin books because they tell so much about other countries."

N.G., Rouyn, Quebec

"Your books offer a world of knowledge about places and people."

L.J. New Orleans, Louisiana

"Your books turn my...life into something quite exciting."

B.M. Baldwin Park, California

"Harlequins take away the world's troubles and for a while you can live in a world of your own where love reigns supreme."

L.S., Beltsville, Maryland

"Thank you for bringing romance back to me."

J.W., Tehachapi, California

"I find Harlequins are the only stories on the market that give me a satisfying romance with sufficient depth without being maudlin."

C.S., Bangor, Maine

"Harlequins are magic carpets...away from pain and depression...away to other people and other countries one might never know otherwise."

H.R., Akron, Ohio

*Names available on request

What readers say about Harlequin Romances

"Your books are the best I have ever found."
P.B.*. Bellevue. Washington

"I enjoy them more and more
with each passing year."
J.L. Spurlockville. West Virginia

"No matter how full and happy life might be,
it is an enchantment to sit
and read your novels."
D.K. Willowdale Ontario

"I firmly believe that Harlequin Romances
are perfect for anyone who wants to read
a good romance."
C.R.. Akron. Ohio

*Names available on request